Sky Birds Dare!

SELECTED FICTION WORKS BY L. RON HUBBARD

FANTASY
The Case of the Friendly Corpse
Death's Deputy
Fear
The Ghoul
The Indigestible Triton
Slaves of Sleep & The Masters of Sleep
Typewriter in the Sky
The Ultimate Adventure

SCIENCE FICTION
Battlefield Earth
The Conquest of Space
The End Is Not Yet
Final Blackout
The Kilkenny Cats
The Kingslayer
The Mission Earth Dekalogy*
Ole Doc Methuselah
To the Stars

ADVENTURE
The Hell Job series

WESTERN
Buckskin Brigades
Empty Saddles
Guns of Mark Jardine
Hot Lead Payoff

A full list of L. Ron Hubbard's
novellas and short stories is provided at the back.

*Dekalogy—a group of ten volumes

L. RON HUBBARD

Sky Birds Dare!

GALAXY
PRESS

Published by
Galaxy Press, LLC
7051 Hollywood Boulevard, Suite 200
Hollywood, CA 90028

© 2011 L. Ron Hubbard Library. All Rights Reserved.

Any unauthorized copying, translation, duplication, importation or distribution, in whole or in part, by any means, including electronic copying, storage or transmission, is a violation of applicable laws.

Mission Earth is a trademark owned by L. Ron Hubbard Library and is used with permission. *Battlefield Earth* is a trademark owned by Author Services, Inc. and is used with permission.

Horsemen illustration from *Western Story Magazine* is © and ™ Condé Nast Publications and is used with their permission. Fantasy, Far-Flung Adventure and Science Fiction illustrations: *Unknown* and *Astounding Science Fiction* © by Street & Smith Publications, Inc. Reprinted with permission of Penny Publications, LLC. Story Preview illustration: *Argosy Magazine* is © 1936 Argosy Communications, Inc. All Rights Reserved. Reprinted with permission of Argosy Communications, Inc.

Printed in the United States of America.

ISBN-10 1-59212-300-7
ISBN-13 978-1-59212-300-1

Library of Congress Control Number: 2007903532

Contents

Foreword	vii
Sky Birds Dare!	1
Story Preview: Trouble on His Wings	81
Glossary	91
L. Ron Hubbard in the Golden Age of Pulp Fiction	97
The Stories from the Golden Age	109

FOREWORD

Stories from Pulp Fiction's Golden Age

AND it *was* a golden age.
The 1930s and 1940s were a vibrant, seminal time for a gigantic audience of eager readers, probably the largest per capita audience of readers in American history. The magazine racks were chock-full of publications with ragged trims, garish cover art, cheap brown pulp paper, low cover prices—and the most excitement you could hold in your hands.

"Pulp" magazines, named for their rough-cut, pulpwood paper, were a vehicle for more amazing tales than Scheherazade could have told in a million and one nights. Set apart from higher-class "slick" magazines, printed on fancy glossy paper with quality artwork and superior production values, the pulps were for the "rest of us," adventure story after adventure story for people who liked to *read*. Pulp fiction authors were no-holds-barred entertainers—real storytellers. They were more interested in a thrilling plot twist, a horrific villain or a white-knuckle adventure than they were in lavish prose or convoluted metaphors.

The sheer volume of tales released during this wondrous golden age remains unmatched in any other period of literary history—hundreds of thousands of published stories in over nine hundred different magazines. Some titles lasted only an

• FOREWORD •

issue or two; many magazines succumbed to paper shortages during World War II, while others endured for decades yet. Pulp fiction remains as a treasure trove of stories you can read, stories you can love, stories you can remember. The stories were driven by plot and character, with grand heroes, terrible villains, beautiful damsels (often in distress), diabolical plots, amazing places, breathless romances. The readers wanted to be taken beyond the mundane, to live adventures far removed from their ordinary lives—and the pulps rarely failed to deliver.

In that regard, pulp fiction stands in the tradition of all memorable literature. For as history has shown, good stories are much more than fancy prose. William Shakespeare, Charles Dickens, Jules Verne, Alexandre Dumas—many of the greatest literary figures wrote their fiction for the readers, not simply literary colleagues and academic admirers. And writers for pulp magazines were no exception. These publications reached an audience that dwarfed the circulations of today's short story magazines. Issues of the pulps were scooped up and read by over thirty million avid readers each month.

Because pulp fiction writers were often paid no more than a cent a word, they had to become prolific or starve. They also had to write aggressively. As Richard Kyle, publisher and editor of *Argosy*, the first and most long-lived of the pulps, so pointedly explained: "The pulp magazine writers, the best of them, worked for markets that did not write for critics or attempt to satisfy timid advertisers. Not having to answer to anyone other than their readers, they wrote about human

• FOREWORD •

beings on the edges of the unknown, in those new lands the future would explore. They wrote for what we would become, not for what we had already been."

Some of the more lasting names that graced the pulps include H. P. Lovecraft, Edgar Rice Burroughs, Robert E. Howard, Max Brand, Louis L'Amour, Elmore Leonard, Dashiell Hammett, Raymond Chandler, Erle Stanley Gardner, John D. MacDonald, Ray Bradbury, Isaac Asimov, Robert Heinlein—and, of course, L. Ron Hubbard.

In a word, he was among the most prolific and popular writers of the era. He was also the most enduring—hence this series—and certainly among the most legendary. It all began only months after he first tried his hand at fiction, with L. Ron Hubbard tales appearing in *Thrilling Adventures, Argosy, Five-Novels Monthly, Detective Fiction Weekly, Top-Notch, Texas Ranger, War Birds, Western Stories,* even *Romantic Range.* He could write on any subject, in any genre, from jungle explorers to deep-sea divers, from G-men and gangsters, cowboys and flying aces to mountain climbers, hard-boiled detectives and spies. But he really began to shine when he turned his talent to science fiction and fantasy of which he authored nearly fifty novels or novelettes to forever change the shape of those genres.

Following in the tradition of such famed authors as Herman Melville, Mark Twain, Jack London and Ernest Hemingway, Ron Hubbard actually lived adventures that his own characters would have admired—as an ethnologist among primitive tribes, as prospector and engineer in hostile

♦ FOREWORD ♦

climes, as a captain of vessels on four oceans. He even wrote a series of articles for *Argosy,* called "Hell Job," in which he lived and told of the most dangerous professions a man could put his hand to.

Finally, and just for good measure, he was also an accomplished photographer, artist, filmmaker, musician and educator. But he was first and foremost a *writer,* and that's the L. Ron Hubbard we come to know through the pages of this volume.

This library of Stories from the Golden Age presents the best of L. Ron Hubbard's fiction from the heyday of storytelling, the Golden Age of the pulp magazines. In these eighty volumes, readers are treated to a full banquet of 153 stories, a kaleidoscope of tales representing every imaginable genre: science fiction, fantasy, western, mystery, thriller, horror, even romance—action of all kinds and in all places.

Because the pulps themselves were printed on such inexpensive paper with high acid content, issues were not meant to endure. As the years go by, the original issues of every pulp from *Argosy* through *Zeppelin Stories* continue crumbling into brittle, brown dust. This library preserves the L. Ron Hubbard tales from that era, presented with a distinctive look that brings back the nostalgic flavor of those times.

L. Ron Hubbard's Stories from the Golden Age has something for every taste, every reader. These tales will return you to a time when fiction was good clean entertainment and

• FOREWORD •

the most fun a kid could have on a rainy afternoon or the best thing an adult could enjoy after a long day at work.

Pick up a volume, and remember what reading is supposed to be all about. Remember curling up with a *great story*.

—Kevin J. Anderson

KEVIN J. ANDERSON *is the author of more than ninety critically acclaimed works of speculative fiction, including* The Saga of Seven Suns, *the continuation of the Dune Chronicles with Brian Herbert, and his* New York Times *bestselling novelization of L. Ron Hubbard's* Ai! Pedrito!

Sky Birds Dare!

CHAPTER ONE

While Other Men Scoff

BREEZE CALLAHAN came into the hangar. He saw two things in the gloom, each one representing an entirely different emotion.

One was his soaring ship, ready for the trial flights.

The other was Badger O'Dowell.

Breeze Callahan swung six feet of brawn into action behind two sets of ferocity-hardened knuckles.

Badger O'Dowell had not been expecting this. He heard the rush of feet behind him. He heard a snarl which reminded him of a mother bear about to protect a foolish cub. And then Badger O'Dowell took off backwards, catapulted by the impact of meeting. Badger O'Dowell did a neat outside loop and then crashed.

For a man built on the proportions of a stuffed sausage, Badger O'Dowell moved very quickly. Dust swirled and he was on his feet. His two protruding eyes searched for the door. When he had oriented himself sufficiently and had directed his footsteps in that direction, Badger O'Dowell discovered too late that Breeze Callahan had all the skyway in that direction.

It was all very unfortunate for Badger O'Dowell. He tried to stop his rush before Breeze Callahan misconstrued his intention, but he could not.

It appeared to the lank tower of shivering, awe-inspiring rage that Badger was charging back to the fray.

Breeze Callahan was very obliging. He set himself. He let go one from the knees and did a spot landing on Badger's chin. Badger completed a wingless soaring record, skidded to a stop in the corner of the hangar and screamed.

"Don't hit me! For God's sake don't hit me!"

But Breeze wasn't a man to enquire deeply into things when his new soaring plane was in question, and he suspected, with very great reason, that Badger O'Dowell had been discovered in the act of sabotage. Breeze advanced and Badger screamed.

Breeze snatched at O'Dowell's collar, and then it became apparent that he had walked into a trap. A six-inch spanner soared up out of the dust, came down and laid open the side of Callahan's face.

Breeze staggered, spouting blood and nerve-shaking oaths. Badger O'Dowell threw the spanner away, leaped to his feet and sprinted for the exit.

Callahan cleared the red film from his eyes. Everything was suddenly zero-zero to him, and he had no beam to guide a blind pilot. He heard a motor snarl into life. He heard gears clash. He heard Badger O'Dowell leave there at about seventy miles an hour.

Which was just as well.

Breeze swabbed his face with some dirty cotton waste, and his curses simmered down to ineffectual, "Dirty so-and-so, lousy bum, good-for-nothing . . ."

Another silhouette appeared in the hangar door. "Hey,

what's going on in here?" said Pop Donegan. "I thought I heard . . . Hell, you're all cut up, Breeze. What happened?"

"That little sawed-off, mangy . . . That guy Badger O'Dowell was in here fooling with the *Chinook*."

Pop Donegan looked up at Breeze. Everybody had to look up at Breeze, and almost anybody had a good chance of looking through him.

Pop Donegan was all concern for the soaring plane, but he smiled—he always smiled—and said optimistically, "Well, he didn't have time to do anything, no matter how much he wanted to."

"Is that so," said Breeze. "Don't stand there looking helpless. Get busy and inspect the thing. My God, the wings are torn off and he's kicked holes in the fuselage, and he's jimmied the controls. . . ."

This was not altogether true, and Breeze was not exactly qualified to pass upon it, as he could not see through the blood which kept coming out of the cut. But he was very certain that these things had happened, and anybody who knew Badger O'Dowell, and who knew just why he hated Breeze Callahan, would have agreed with Breeze without further remark.

Pop Donegan looked at the soaring ship, with his hands in his pockets. To inspect it thoroughly a man would have to crawl under it and somehow—because of rheumatism, Pop said—he never crawled under anything that looked like work. Pop shifted a healthy chew, spat so that a small geyser leaped out of the dust, and cocked his head on one side.

"She looks all right, Breeze. Perfectly all right."

By this time Breeze had gotten to a water faucet and had thrust his head into the tub beneath, and by buckling his helmet tight, he managed to keep his sight clear. He rambled over to the *Chinook* and began to run practiced fingers over the sleek wings and frail body of the motorless plane.

After a little he was satisfied that Badger O'Dowell had done nothing wrong. Breeze stood up straight, lighted a cigarette and leaned on the cockpit.

"Have they come yet?"

"Patty came a little while ago. She's trying to start the tow car for you. Oh, don't you worry, Breeze. They'll be along directly. We've waited and worked for months over this thing, and they won't stay away now. And we can't fail this time. No sir, we can't fail. Why with you at the *Chinook*'s controls, them Navy fellers will see that a soaring plane can do things a power plane never thought of doing, and then we'll be all set."

"Hmph," said Breeze, dragging smoke into his lungs. "I haven't had her off for a week and there's plenty of wind today. I wish they'd get here. I'm nervous."

"Now you just calm yourself, Breeze. They can't help but think that this is the finest thing which has happened in the way of training. I'm willing to bet you . . ."

Voices came from outside. Breeze stood up straight and rambled toward the door.

A somewhat harsh voice, roughened by fine cigars in quantity, said, "I know, I know, the boy may be right, but this fellow O'Dowell has a mighty fine proposition in training ships, you know. They'll do all this work and more."

"We'll watch it anyway," said another.

"Yeah," said the harsh voice. "We'll watch it. I like to get out on days like these anyway. Too much office. But I still say that gliding is a sport and nothing more. Kid stuff, in fact. No possible use in training whatever. Where's the man in charge here?"

Breeze came out of the hangar. He looked over his three visitors. They were Naval officers, but they were not in uniform. They had a lean, spray-whipped look about them. Even in felt hats they looked seagoing. Two of them were young. The third was elderly and fatherly. He offered Breeze a cigar.

"I'm Captain Daniels, young man. This is Lieutenant Sweeney and this is Lieutenant Maynard, both of the Bureau of Aeronautics. Who's in charge around here?"

"I am," said Breeze.

Captain Daniels looked at him for several seconds. Captain Daniels was not impressed. Breeze was dressed in greasy coveralls and a helmet without goggles. Breeze looked rather southern and lazy and he drawled a little. Definitely not a military man, this Callahan. But a nice looking boy.

Captain Daniels was hearty. "Well, son, you've got us out here, now what are you going to do with us?"

"I want to show you how the *Chinook* can fly," said Breeze. "She's the last word in motorless aircraft, gentlemen. She's a smooth ship. Fifty-five-foot spread, with a wing loading of—"

"How do you do?" said Captain Daniels over Breeze's shoulder.

Patty Donegan had come up. The interest of the two lieutenants quickened instantly. Patty looked very fresh and young. The wind was getting under her small brown hat and pulling at her corn-colored hair, and she was having some trouble keeping it out of her very large, clear blue eyes.

"Are you all ready?" said Patty, smiling at the lieutenants.

Breeze looked at Patty and frowned. He looked at the lieutenants and frowned.

"Yes, indeed," said Captain Daniels. The lieutenants beamed, as Navy pilots will do when they see a girl who impresses them.

In spite of his annoyance, Breeze said, "I wanted to tell you about this first, gentlemen. I understand that the Navy is not satisfied with its present training routine at Pensacola. It's an opinion of mine that power pilots are likely to be improved when they are given training on soaring planes. Now it happens that I have designed this *Chinook* ruggedly enough for a training ship without impairing its capabilities in soaring, and I would like—"

"By the way," said Captain Daniels, "do you know a fellow named O'Dowell? Yes? Well, he was over to see us this morning and he spoke very highly of you. Fine chap, this fellow O'Dowell. He has a small trainer which we were thinking of using on our next contract. He says it gives you the feel of the air."

"Is that so?" said Breeze.

"Yes, and he was most sympathetic toward your gliders. Said they were the finest of their kind. But of course gliders are limited. He told us—"

"Shall I run her out?" yelled Pop Donegan from the hangar.

Breeze went down, too angry at O'Dowell to be surprised

at Pop's offer. Together they trundled the soaring ship out into the sunshine.

She was a beautiful thing, that plane. Her wings were so thin that you could see the sunlight through them, and yet they were strong. The body was graceful and tapering. She was silver. Breeze, with his clever hands, had built a certain swagger into her lines, and although at first glance the *Chinook* appeared to be just one more monoplane, motorless plane, any bystander was instantly impressed.

Captain Daniels was very polite. He looked into the small cockpit and he felt of the fabric. The two lieutenants were interested only because Patty began to point things out to them.

Patty smiled and laughed with them. "Yes, I've flown it and it's wonderful. Balances perfectly. Picks up lift from the most amazing places. Breeze stayed up over an hour in her about a week ago when he was setting the . . ."

They were not interested in Breeze, those lieutenants. They changed the subject.

Breeze alone showed any strain. He knew how much this meant. If he could put on a fine flight for them and show them something about soaring, he had a chance of convincing them of the possibilities of such a thing, and if he did, they might use sailplanes at Pensacola for regular training, and if they did that, then Breeze Callahan would pinch pennies no more. And Patty Donegan's rather passive interest in him would quicken until . . .

Breeze eased his length into the cockpit and pulled the hood down. Other than its lack of a motor, this might have been any monoplane. But the lack was a gain in Breeze's eyes. He could see nothing but soaring and motors were so much racket in his ears. He liked the silent, delicate flight of a glider, and above them all, he loved the way *Chinook* whispered down the skies.

Pop Donegan excitedly connected the towrope to the back of the old rattletrap car, and then hooked the other end to the release on the *Chinook*'s nose. The plane was headed into the strong wind and Pop began to take up the slack by moving the car away.

The rope was about six hundred feet long. When it was stretched, Pop looked back. Breeze glanced at Patty and saw she was still talking with the lieutenants. Captain Daniels was sitting on the ground, chewing a straw and watching without any great interest. Pop Donegan caught Breeze's signal, spat and shoved the car into low.

The *Chinook* gave a lurch and rolled ahead on its one wheel. Breeze shifted the stick, picked up the down wing and balanced the plane. Pop began to roll faster. The *Chinook* scuttled along the ground, controls getting stiffer as the wind sucked up against the wings.

Pop had the automobile in high, grinding out forty miles an hour over the bumpy field. The *Chinook* took the air.

Breeze hauled back on the stick. The rope was taut, pulling hard. The ship went up the invisible staircase to the clouds.

Wind whispered through the struts and sang over Breeze's head. He forgot about Patty and the lieutenants. He was thinking about what he could do with soaring planes, if they would let him.

Swiftly he completed the climb. The motive power furnished by the car was no longer needed now. The car and Pop were six hundred feet straight down and the rope was still tight. Pop was looking up and hitting the bumps hard.

Breeze pulled the rope release. The long snake whipped out of sight to the rear, falling in loose coils. Pop stopped the car and looked up, watching the wings, through which he could see the sun.

Twenty feet forward to one foot down. That was the gliding angle of the *Chinook*. You could coast down twenty miles, if you started a mile high. Something like a kid's wagon on the hill, and the air under the wings was as solid as concrete.

Breeze looked back at the hangar. He could hear cars traveling along the road. He could hear voices far off. He was above it all, and away from it. He was a solitary eagle in the clouds.

He was free from the earth and all the man-made woes. He felt exultant. He looked down again and saw that a car was parked along a woods road behind the field. With a start, he knew that it was Badger O'Dowell's.

Well, let the so-and-so watch if it would do him any good. Let him watch a good flight.

Breeze knew that the wind struck the side of the hill and shot upwards. He knew that these bumps in the air, so annoying to the power pilot, were the breath of life of motorless aircraft. The air hit the under side of the spreading wings and boosted the ship bodily.

He banked gracefully. He could be nothing but graceful up

there. He was part of the plane. The wings were not attached to the fuselage but to his own shoulders. The wind which caressed his face was his own, personal, untainted property.

He hit a bump. He felt heavy in the pit as the plane rose suddenly. He was back to six hundred feet. He banked again and rode along the crest of the hill. Again he went up. He was showing them what a power pilot had to learn.

Back he went along the crest, sighing through space—flying as great birds have flown since the beginning of time. Flying without moving a wing or using any power, merely relying upon the lift of the wind on wings.

He came back over the field. He had plenty of time. He dived steeply and did a quick bank which made the earth spin. He pulled the stick back toward neutral. And then—

Then his whole being felt empty.

The *Chinook* was not answering. The stick was stuck hard over. His wings were dipped to five o'clock and he could look straight ahead and see the earth which rushed at him.

He was spinning and he could do nothing about it. He had only a few hundred feet to recover and that was not enough. The *Chinook,* that fragile thing of linen and spruce which he had been months in building, was about to smash out his life against the hard earth.

Gliding was dangerous. Yes, he knew that. But he didn't expect that *his* ship, *his Chinook* would hurt him.

In a mounting crescendo, the wind shrilled by the wings. The fabric began to shiver under this great speed.

But it took a long, long time to fall. He had a lot of time. Lots of time.

O'Dowell. That was it. Badger O'Dowell. There were stories about that man. He had once owned a large aircraft factory, but that was gone. He was trying to make a comeback by selling the Navy light training planes powered with small motors.

O'Dowell was doing this to him.

There were ugly things said. In his war days, O'Dowell had worked with the first chutes. After the war O'Dowell had packed another man's parachute and sewn the rip cord with safety wire. When the other man had jumped, his chute never left the bag. That other man had fallen six thousand feet, had fallen free, and had been smashed into a self-dug grave all because O'Dowell . . .

And now the *Chinook* . . .

He hit and did not know that he had hit. His ears rang and he sat feebly up, dizzy and stunned. The wings of the silver *Chinook* were crumpled like paper about him.

Patty and Pop were coming.

Breeze lifted himself up and then remembered his safety belt. He unbuckled it and crawled out, but he could not stand.

"What happened?" yelled Pop.

Patty lifted Breeze to his feet. There was pity in her clear blue eyes.

"I'll . . . I'll build another," said Breeze. "O'Dowell must have jammed an aileron. I'll . . . I'll build another and then we'll show . . ."

Captain Daniels came up and saw that Breeze was not hurt. Captain Daniels looked over the wreck and looked back at his lieutenants who were somewhat envious of Breeze's sudden limelight.

O'Dowell was doing this to him.

"Young man," said Captain Daniels to Breeze, "young man, when you learn how to fly that thing, write me another letter. I like to get away from the office afternoons. Come on, gentlemen."

Breeze stared after them. His lean jaw set.

One of the lieutenants looked back and smiled at Patty. The other one looked back at the *Chinook*.

"Kid stuff," somebody said.

"We'll see," muttered Breeze.

CHAPTER TWO

Pop Talks Blimps

A hangar is an especially gloomy place on a rainy day. Rain makes you think of some poor devil coming down the skies with the earth shut away from him, hoping his gas will last until he can see his way through to land.

There is something sad about rain on a flying field. The ships sit very still, with motors swathed in canvas, and recede into the gloom of hangars. Outside, the water stands in puddles and you know that even when the sun comes out, the ground will be too soggy to support the wheels for a takeoff.

True to form as a pilot, Breeze Callahan felt blue. He sat just inside the door of the small office and stared at the lowering clouds. In the barnlike depths he could see his *Chinook,* still a mass of ripped fabric. That too made him sad. He did not have enough money to rebuild the *Chinook* and all his immediate hopes for soaring into the hearts of the Navy powers that be were lying there, just as shattered as the sailplane.

He had not seen Patty for two days. Perhaps she saw only too clearly that a man whose talents and time were all taken up by "kid stuff" was hardly a fit object for a husband.

As though called in by his thought, Patty stepped through the door. The rain meant nothing to her. The blonde hair was tangled and damp and raindrops stood out on her cheeks.

She took off her small hat and threw it down on the desk. Then, without saying a word, sensing Breeze's preoccupation, she swung herself up to the counter and sat there quietly.

After a long time she said, "I've got to run down to Washington this afternoon, Breeze darling. The old bus is flooded out and I was wondering if you'd start it for me."

"Sure," said Breeze absently without looking at her. Then the light quickened in his glance and he whirled to face her. He saw that she wore her poor best under the old slicker.

"Washington?" said Breeze. "Maybe those lieutenants . . ."

"Don't be silly," said Patty. "You're in a spin, Breeze darling. Those lieutenants—"

"Eat little girls at a gulp," finished Breeze. "Stay away from them."

"But I wasn't . . ." Patty stared at him for several seconds, puzzled.

Breeze, in the zero-zero depths of his mood, took the stare for a glare. Patty looked beautiful, sitting there. Fragile and graceful, like the *Chinook*.

His glance wandered to the crumpled mass of silver fabric which had been the sailplane. Suddenly he was filled with bitterness. Patty had no right to sit there and look like that.

"Go on and snare those tailor's dummies," said Breeze. "Go on and see if I care."

Patty moved restlessly. Some evil fiend within her said, "Oh, I don't know. I thought they were quite nice."

That was the first salvo. Breeze stood up, facing her, hands clenched at his sides. His pride was hurt, after the late experience with the *Chinook*, and now Patty . . .

"That's like a woman," said Breeze. "Go ahead and ditch me just because I'm down. Go ahead and run off with somebody else and see if I care. I guess I can get along. One of these days I'll get enough money to put that sailplane together and you'll be sorry!"

With that, Breeze sat down again and stared out at the rain. "Go on and start the bus yourself."

Patty's feelings were hurt, but she had been raised in the flying game. She had been with men all her life. She would not sit quietly.

"That's it, sulk," said Patty. "Sit there and sulk. If you had any manhood in you, you'd get busy and do something real. You've been moping around about gliding, why don't you get out and show the world what it's all about for a change. Or haven't you got the nerve? If I was you, I'd quit it. I'd get me a job I was fitted for like . . . like street cleaning."

Breeze clenched his hands. "So you think that way too, do you? So you think I've failed. Well . . . I don't care what you think."

"Here you could get a job with any aircraft plant as a designer," said Patty in a voice which stabbed. "You could make a decent living. But no, you'd rather play around with sailplanes all your life. If I didn't know you better, I'd think you were just plain lazy. In fact, you *are* lazy."

"I am not!" cried Breeze. "If you talk about that, you'd better look to your old man."

"You leave him out of this."

"Yeah?" said Breeze. "Yeah?"

"Yeah."

Patty got up and went to the door, but she did not leave. Before she could touch the knob it came inward and Pop Donegan entered the room, dripping but smiling as usual.

Pop Donegan did not know that a battle was in progress, or if he did, he took the advantage of a neutral state. He had a folder in his hands which was somewhat damaged by the rain.

"Look here," said Pop. "Look here, Breeze. This is the business we ought to be in."

He handled the paper reverently. "Look, it says a blimp is coming to town to take up people and they're going to charge five dollars a ride. That's the business we ought to be in. Listen, if you had a blimp at five dollars a ride and you took up five hundred people in a day, you'd get twenty-five hundred dollars, and the cost wouldn't be fifty."

Breeze was annoyed. He had known Pop Donegan for many years. Pop was one of the originals in flying. Pop had flown shortly after the Wright brothers, and then had changed over to the promoting end of it. Pop had done everything in flying that could be done by way of promoting. He had not sufficient business sense, however, to long remain on top of the pile—but he dreamed some wonderful dreams.

"Five dollars a ride," sighed Pop putting the folder down on the counter. "We could make some real money. . . . Say, listen, Breeze, why don't you and me sort of slide in on some of that money?"

Breeze managed a polite, "How?"

"Look here," said Pop. "You remember what they used to do with the *Akron* and *Macon*. They used to drop planes out of them. Well, I don't recall offhand that anybody ever dropped a glider out of a dirigible."

"And probably never will," said Patty. "It's dumb."

"I don't think so," said Breeze in a slow voice. "Go on, Pop."

Pop warmed to his task. "Listen, if you was to get some store to give you some handbills to drop, and if we was to tie in with this blimp and arrange to take some of their five dollars, we might be able to get enough money together to rebuild the *Chinook*."

"Say—" began Breeze.

"What will you use for a glider?" said Patty coldly.

"The old utility ship we've got back there," said Breeze promptly.

Patty's mouth opened a little. "But it's all apart and the wings are full of holes. That thing won't fly."

"Sure it will," said Breeze. "I'll make it fly."

"Attaboy," said Pop.

"But you're liable to be . . ." Patty turned her back then and went out to the bus. She called, "Go ahead, Mister Breeze. I'll give your regards to the lieutenants."

Breeze's nostrils flared. He turned to Pop and looked most ferocious. "We'll get these guys when they come in tomorrow morning," said Breeze. "I'll do the drop over the city of Washington and land down on the Speedway. That's an idea, Pop, that's an idea."

Pop grinned and went to the phone. Pop knew how to get things when he wanted them badly enough.

CHAPTER THREE

Treachery—Badger O'Dowell's Style

BEFORE, it had been an aileron. Before, it had been a small knot in the control cable which had locked in a pulley. Before, the *Chinook* had canted over at five o'clock to go whistling down at the earth.

What would it be this time?

Breeze was quite confident of his luck. He knew that it was bad. And knowing that, all he could do was make a few provisions and wonder about it.

"O'Dowell," said Breeze, "hasn't landed that training plane contract yet?"

"No," said Pop, looking up at the silver bulk of the blimp. "No, not yet, but they say it won't be long. It's all a question of bids. If we could really interest those fellers in sailplanes—"

"Hey, down there," said a man in the blimp's gondola. "You better be getting ready."

"Sure," said Breeze and began to check the ancient utility ship for the tenth time.

He had made himself a hook dead center above the wings, a sort of cabane, as near the center of gravity as possible. From this the utility ship would dangle like some crazy pendulum until Breeze yanked the release mechanism which would drop him down through the sky.

He had it very nicely figured, all of it, but many an engineer has built a fine building only to discover that the site is quicksand.

The old sailplane had once been silver. Now it had mellowed to the color of parchment. The once bright wires were brown with rust, and the fabric fluttered in the faint wind. It was not exactly a cheerful sight, that utility ship. It made you sad, as though it told you not to be so snooty, you'd be old and worn some day, too.

It was another *Chinook* of older pattern. It had a cockpit with a hood over it. It had one wing with a forty-five-foot spread, and it looked like an obsolete motorless airplane.

The license had expired some time before. It carried a large experimental X now. Only that. The Department of Commerce cares very little what happens to gliders and gliders' pilots. Let them kill themselves and save something else the trouble. Let sailplanes fly until they fell apart in the air, that was all right. Nobody cares about a sailplane. Kid stuff, soaring.

If a person had no better sense than to fly motorless heavier-than-air stuff, then that wasn't the government's fault. What was a soaring plane but a toy? The thing went up a few hundred feet, sailed around in the air without bothering anybody and then, obeying gravity at last, sailed down to the ground. Soaring planes never went anywhere or did anything. Good way for fools to amuse themselves. If there weren't soaring planes, then there would be that many more power pilots with weak brains.

Oh, there were rumors at that time that somebody in Germany had done some odd things with ships which had no motors, but Germany was different. At that time the treaties were still in force. Germany could have no power planes. And Germany's youth had made a business of sailplanes. In Germany it was a fine art, but everybody knew that if you gave a glider pilot a chance at power, he would instantly desert his silent flight.

These riders of the wind flew sailplanes because they were too poor to do anything else, that was all.

What? Risk your neck in something which didn't even have a motor? Let somebody else do that, said the power pilots. Let somebody else trust their lives to clouds. *They* wanted motors when they flew.

And nobody even cared to find out just what you could do with a glider.

People had forgotten that the Wrights flew gliders first. That Leonardo da Vinci designed them. That the natives of South America's hinterland were said to fly long before the coming of the Spaniards.

Interesting, but we had gasoline now.

A motorless plane, that poor utility ship, was dwarfed beside this commercial blimp. The plane was not much bigger than the gasbag's gondola. An engineer was working on a motor inside. From time to time he looked down pityingly upon the sailplane.

Breeze Callahan finished his inspection. No Navy men had come down this day. The Navy was not interested in killing off their pilots so easily. Pursuit ships were dangerous enough. Only Pop Donegan was there. Patty was somewhere in town, maybe seeing the lieutenants.

Breeze tested the hook again. Too bad if that let go before

he was ready up there. No more Breeze Callahan if that happened. And he couldn't afford to buy a chute.

"How much are we getting?" said Breeze.

"Eight hundred dollars in all," said Pop, "but that ain't anything when you think of the publicity. You'll be on all the front pages today."

The blimp commander was a young man. He had barnstormed until his eyes were old. He knew commercial value, he knew what drew the crowds. He knew that this exhibition would bring him more passengers than he had ever had before. They would see the ship over Washington, they would see the glider dive away from the silver belly of the gasbag, they would see . . . Well, maybe it would be better if Breeze made a fine flight of it.

"All set there?"

Breeze nodded. Pop Donegan stood by a wing, and the blimp commander gave some orders to a ground crew. Breeze climbed into his cockpit and drew the hood up until all you could see was a greasy helmet and his eyes.

The gasbag was lifting in the hot wind. The crew maneuvered it until the gondola was just over the top of the glider. The hook snapped into place.

The engine began to roar overhead. The glider jerked as it came away from the ground. Breeze looked down and saw Pop fifty feet under him.

Breeze looked up. He could see the gondola's keel, that was all. He was hanging under a silver cloud, all alone and sailing. The hook held very well.

The Potomac began to even out with distance. The

Washington Monument stood up like a tombstone. The Capitol glittered in the afternoon sunlight.

Patty was down there someplace with the lieutenants.

Breeze shifted uneasily. This was an odd thing. He had been attached to the ground many times by means of a tow rope. Never before had he hung from a silver cloud in the sky.

The wind was coming from the west. He would have to make a steep dive of it to get down to the Speedway from two thousand feet. He didn't have any motor to compensate for a bad bit of judgment. One error in distance calculation and he would get himself a ducking in the Potomac.

They were fifteen hundred feet up. Breeze felt his controls. They were going pretty fast in the blimp. Made the utility plane buck against its hook as the wind tried to make it fly of its own accord.

Down below, L'Enfant's surveying work was laid out in miniature. The whole city was a hub, radiating from the Capitol. The streets were black and crawling. Faces were turned up. People looked funny down there.

Suddenly great snowflakes came down about him. The handbills. One of them fell into his lap and he read, "Buy now! Summer values . . . Woodward and Hahn's Department Store . . ."

Wind was rumpling his escaped locks. He felt happy. Eight hundred would let him repair the *Chinook,* and then he'd show them.

A face was jutting out of the gondola over his head. Something in Breeze turned over.

O'Dowell!

The man was grinning. The blimp's engine wasn't loud and the wind did not carry away his words.

"Hello, Breeze," he said.

Breeze looked at the hook and then down at the ground. The blimp was over the Capitol now. Too far west. He wouldn't get back to the Speedway. What was the matter with that commander up there? Didn't he know that the glider would hit the river and that Breeze . . . ?

The handbills were still showering down toward the streets. Good advertisement, those. People were watching.

O'Dowell withdrew his head. The commander looked out and down.

"Let her go!" shouted the commander.

Breeze shook his head and pointed at the river. His voice wouldn't carry up, but the commander's could come down.

There were two releases up there. They could drop the glider if they . . .

With a grating rasp, the hook parted.

The plane swooped down.

Breeze snatched at the controls and raced out in level flight. There was something thrilling about this. He had two thousand feet. He had lots of time. He could soar . . .

The river was there, waiting for him unless he dived for Anacostia Naval Station. The field there looked inviting, and the wind was carrying him faster than he thought.

He was over southeast Washington. No use to try for the Speedway. Coming up against the wind, he would have a hard time making the Naval Station. He couldn't dive this glider. The wings were too frail. If he only had the *Chinook* . . .

*With a grating rasp, the hook parted.
The plane swooped down.*

Breeze sideslipped, and the wind fanned his cheek. He leveled out and sideslipped again. Lots of time. He had to kill this altitude somehow.

With rudder and stick he went around and around, volplaning. In spite of this old ship's stiff feel, it was fun.

The blimp was growing small above him. Men on the Naval station were standing and watching. Breeze knew he had better start a straight glide for that field. The Navy had rules about commercial craft, but a glider was in the same category as a sailing ship. It had right-of-way.

And then Breeze saw something else. A squadron of planes were taking off, one by one, from the field. A bomber was landing at Bolling.

He stared with disbelief.

He couldn't sit down in all that mess of wings and engines. He'd crash into somebody and get killed.

Didn't they see him?

Certainly, but who expected him to head for there. They forgot he had no engine. He couldn't make the Speedway against the wind, and they were only mildly interested in this sailplane which went down the skies without an engine. *They* were *power* pilots. They had no use for engineless steeds.

Nothing for it, thought Breeze, coasting above the river. He would have to take his chance in landing on one of those concrete aprons. He would cruise in low over the water. He would touch the surface just as he reached the ramps . . .

What were they going to say there? Maybe they'd be sore about it. And maybe this would wreck any chance of selling the Navy on gliders.

Damn that blimp for dropping him.

But he had no choice. He was risking his life in touching the water and then the ramps. He was coming fast, too fast. He had decided on another place too late.

He slipped. They knew he was coming now. They were running away from the spot. Small blue ants, scurrying.

He slipped again. He was coming too fast. He was lancing toward those hangars at forty miles an hour—twice too fast.

He wanted to laugh then. A man in gold-braided blue was waving him away. As if he could turn now. He had no engine.

He skimmed the surface of the rippling river, heading for the concrete ramps. He could hear men yelling.

His wheel touched water. He pulled up sharply. His wheel touched again. Only a few feet to go, and he was traveling fast enough to upend himself if he touched water.

The nose went down. It was as if he had stubbed his toe at a dead run.

The glider cartwheeled through a geyser of spray. Fabric ripped. Metal rasped.

Breeze unfastened his belt and dropped out of the reversed cockpit.

The utility plane was crumpled like a popped paper bag there on the tarmac. Breeze was trying to calm his nerves. That had been close. Too close. He had almost smashed out his brains on that hard concrete.

The blue ants were running at him. He felt silly somehow, standing there where he didn't belong. He felt apologetic for being alive.

An officer stopped in front of him and snarled, "What the

hell's the idea? This is a Navy field, you idiot. What's the idea of cluttering up the tarmac. . . ."

Breeze stared at him. It was Lieutenant Maynard.

"So it's you," said Maynard. "Who told you to pull this stunt, huh? I've got enough trouble now, without having you come along and . . ."

Other officers were there, looking at the glider. They were somewhat surprised that Maynard would be so hard on a pilot who had just crashed and then they remembered that this was just a soaring pilot and who cared about one of those.

Breeze turned and picked up a wing, trying to turn the wreck around. He did not know why he did it.

Maybe he didn't want Maynard to see his face.

Funny about glider pilots.

Sometimes you lose all patience with them.

Maybe it's because they sit up there in silence and watch the clouds and patterned earth.

Maybe a motor dulls your feelings.

Glider pilots are fools. Breeze knew he was a fool. But he hated to see that poor old sailplane wounded there, crumpled up before those hostile eyes.

Patty was standing just inside the hangar door, watching him.

CHAPTER FOUR

A Proposition—and a Fade-Out

POP DONEGAN was the supreme optimist. He sat on a box watching Breeze work on the *Chinook*. Watching people work was one of Pop's favorite pastimes.

"Sure, and then we'll go up the ridge where there's lots of wind along those cliffs and we'll turn you loose and you can get the American record for endurance. That'll make 'em sit up and take notice, my boy."

Breeze, in spattered overalls, was replacing a crooked rib in the thin wing. "I hope you're right," he said listlessly.

"Oh, don't let it get you down, Breeze. Of course they didn't want you to crack up on their tarmac. Nobody wants anybody to crack up. If they was nasty, just put it down to meanness, that's all. We got the eight hundred, didn't we?"

"Yes, we got that."

"And we'll have the *Chinook*, won't we?"

"Yes."

"And we're still alive, ain't we?"

"Yes."

"Well, what the hell are you worrying about?"

Breeze looked at the hangar door and almost said "Patty." He said, instead, "O'Dowell."

"Aw, why worry about that rat? All he did was tell the

blimp commander you was ready before you were, that's all. He just took a ride and you didn't get hurt and he was just out his money. Don't think about O'Dowell. Why, one of these days that feller will have to stand before you with his hat off and say 'yessir!' He ain't worth worryin' about, Breeze."

Breeze finished the rib and began to haul a billowy fabric covering over the wing, ready to dope it. Pop looked at the paint cans and then at the blue sky through the hangar door and got down off his seat.

"I think I'll see if the bus is okay, Breeze."

Breeze gave him a knowing grin and went on working. Pop drifted outside whistling.

An hour later, Breeze thought that Pop had come back and he didn't bother to look up. The shadow was short. It came on in the hangar and sat down on a sawhorse.

"Callahan."

Breeze glanced up, startled. He felt the hair on his neck rise. O'Dowell was sitting there, paring his nails with a jackknife.

"Get out," said Breeze, in a low voice.

"Callahan, I've come over here to say something to you."

"Get out," said Breeze, juggling a wrench in a sweaty palm.

O'Dowell gave him a crooked grin. "You might as well listen. You're washed up."

"Yeah?"

"Yeah, washed up. I was down to the Navy Department this morning talking to Captain Daniels. He's a pretty nice old guy, isn't he?"

"Maybe you don't hear very well," said Breeze.

"He told me," said O'Dowell, elaborately trimming a nail,

"he told me that he thought you were one of the funniest guys he'd ever met. And he added that he never wanted anything to do with gliders after you'd crashed a couple for his benefit."

"Go on," said Breeze.

"But he said that there were a couple officers higher than him that still had dizzy ideas about sailplanes, even though they would get rid of them just as soon as they read Daniels' report."

"So you came down here. . . ."

"I came down here to make you a proposition," said O'Dowell. "I'll give you one of my small training ships and you can start a school on this field and make yourself some money."

Breeze blinked.

"No strings attached," said O'Dowell, gravely. "I'll give you full title to the ship and all you have to do is leave sailplanes alone. I'm doing this because I like you, Breeze. I don't want you to get hurt."

"No, of course not," said Breeze.

"Of course not."

"And now," said Breeze, "get out."

O'Dowell smiled evilly as he put his knife away. He said, "You'd better change your mind, if you don't want to be wrecked entirely."

"That's a threat?"

"Yes, that's a threat."

"Okay," said Breeze, advancing. "Okay."

O'Dowell backed up, going faster and faster. He whirled and ran for the entrance. Breeze was close behind him. O'Dowell tripped and fell and Breeze, with an effortless motion, picked him up by the collar and towed him across the field to his parked car.

O'Dowell whined and struggled, and his heels dragged up dust. Breeze shoved him in under the wheel and slammed the door.

"There's the road," said Breeze. "I can't stop you from using it. But this field happens to be under lease to me. Remember that."

"You try anything," said O'Dowell between set teeth. "You just try anything with that sailplane and you'll be a dead man."

Breeze left O'Dowell struggling with his gear shift.

He entered the hangar still burning with honest rage, ready to tackle anything. He had progressed halfway across the dirt floor before he saw that he had another visitor.

Patty, struggling in overalls some four sizes too large for her, was industriously beginning to mix dope in five gallon cans.

Breeze stopped and stared at her. This was unexpected. He had not seen Patty for several days and he had not spoken to her for over a week, and yet here she was, without any prelude or apology, going to work on the *Chinook*.

"It ought to be thicker," said Breeze.

"Don't tell *me* how to mix dope."

Breeze grinned and went back to the wing fabric. It was almost finished except for smearing on that peculiar mixture of banana oil and pigment which would tighten the covering until it would roll like a drum when touched.

Patty kept sweeping the blond hair out of her eyes until she had finally stiffened a lock or two with the dope. Then she got some on her nose and successfully smeared the overalls. Finally she was ready to go to work.

They took the brushes in silence and the only sound in the hangar was the slop-slop of wet bristles on linen. After an hour, the wing was silver again.

Patty sat down on a sawbuck and thoughtfully gnawed the end of her brush. Breeze sat down beside her.

"Pretty good job," said Patty after a while.

"Yeah, pretty good. Just so they line up. I'll test her out tomorrow if it's nice."

"I'll come down early and we'll get the quiet air," said Patty. "You can't tell anything when the wind's up."

"That's right," said Breeze. He yawned peacefully. "Hungry? Let's go up to the hash house and eat."

Shortly after that, Patty had succeeded in removing the stubborn dope from her silky skin and returned from the locker room, looking very cheerful.

Breeze put on a coat for form's sake and together they went up toward the parking line, where Patty had parked her ancient, wheezy roadster.

A long yellow car was sitting there and a shiny-faced young man was sitting in it, smoking a cigarette. It was Lieutenant Sweeney.

"Hello," said the lieutenant. "Forget you had a date with me, Patty?"

Patty blushed and looked at the ground. "I . . . guess so. You better forget it, Jim."

"Forget it? No, a date's a date, young lady. You said to meet you out here at five and it's five-thirty now. Come on, get in."

"No thanks," said Patty, giving him a rather cold smile after recovering her poise. "I've changed my mind."

She turned toward Breeze, but Breeze wasn't there. Breeze had vanished completely.

Patty's eyes blazed as she glared at Sweeney. "You'd better get out of here," she said. "You'd better get out before . . . before . . . No, that's all right. I'll go with you."

CHAPTER FIVE

Trailing at Ninety Miles an Hour

BREEZE coasted down the wind, picked up some lift from a fence, coasted again and skimmed in for a perfect landing. He pushed back the *Chinook*'s hood and pulled off his greasy helmet.

Pop brought the tow car back under the uplifted sailship's wing, "How's she go, Breeze?"

Breeze grinned with justifiable pride. "Better than ever. That aileron adjustment was just what it needed. Sweet as a bird, Pop. I feel like one of those buzzards up there."

For several seconds he gazed at the black silhouettes soaring effortlessly over a line of trees, drifting without the motion of a wing.

"You know," said Breeze, "if I could soar like they do, I'd be willing to eat what they do."

Pop made a face. "That ain't delicate."

"I mean it, though," said Breeze.

Pop looked at this lanky sailplane pilot basking in his pit and decided the time had come to break the news.

"Breeze, what are you and me trying to do?"

"I guess we're trying to blackjack the Navy into buying a few dozen planes from us," said Breeze.

"That's it. And what progress have we made so far?"

Breeze's face fell a little. "None."

"No, the trouble is this," said Pop. "We ain't been getting the publicity we should have been getting, that's what. You know if we was to do something which would make all the papers spread us on the first page, them fellers up there at the Navy Department would see it and that would be that. They'd say, 'Well, them things do amount to something after all.'"

"Hear, hear," said Breeze. "What the hell do you think I've been risking my neck for, huh? And how much publicity have we gotten?"

"You don't get it," said Pop. "I've got me a fine idea." He paused, suspecting that Breeze would laugh at him, but Breeze was only attentive.

"It isn't," said Pop, "exactly my idea. But I had an offer this morning which I think we ought to take. We'll call off this soaring endurance stunt and grab off this thing."

"What is it?"

"Sky train," said Pop. "A sky train." He grew pretty excited about it and climbed out of the tow car and crouched beside the pit. "Listen, Breeze, they've done it in Russia, and we ought to do it here."

"Yeah, but where we going to get the dough?"

Pop beamed. "It's all set. There's a bunch of these phil . . . phil . . ."

"Stamp collectors?"

"Yep, that's it. Stamp collectors. And there's a feller that thinks it would be good publicity for him personally. He saw me this morning. Johnson is his name. He's got a small ship and he'll fly it himself and he wants a couple of gliders to tack on behind and he's going to fly from here down to Miami and from Miami over to Havana, and he wants you to fly the *Chinook* like that, towed by an airplane. He can get a sack of mail from the Post Office Department and some new stamps and everything."

Breeze grinned and stepped out of the sailplane. "When do we leave?" he said.

They left within the week, much to Breeze's delight. Breeze was not a man to be long inactive and he was anxious to get everything straightened out. He fondly believed that when the Navy saw this stunt they would believe that a warplane could tow a spy in a glider over enemy lines and then let the fellow loose to drift down silently into enemy territory.

It was a good idea, another selling point. Maybe this would wipe out those past two mistakes, and maybe Patty would see him in a better light.

The nerve of that girl Patty. Here he'd known her since they had been small enough to fit together behind one safety belt and now—he couldn't really believe it—she was attracted by some eggs who wore gold braid.

Breeze met the other glider pilot. The fellow was a German named Grauer. Breeze had heard of the man. The fellow had made several soaring records in Europe.

Grauer was a square built man, blond and silent, with eyes for nothing but wings.

They flipped a coin for first place and Grauer won. Johnson did not care how they settled it. Johnson was only thinking about getting high prices for these canceled stamps, he said.

Although three men in such an enterprise might be expected to show some signs of companionship and excitement, Breeze felt a certain hostility in the group.

Grauer never had anything to say. Johnson never smiled. Johnson was about Breeze's height, but he was black haired and somehow greasy. He thought about the money end of it far too much to suit Breeze.

The morning they turned out in the dawn to get ready for the takeoff, Pop approached Breeze with a dismal expression on his face.

"Listen, Breeze, maybe you better pull out of this."

Breeze was startled. He looked at Pop's thin face, which drifted in the fog before him.

"Breeze, did you look at the ship which was going to pull you?"

Breeze shook his head and stepped closer to the power plane. He scowled. "An O'Dowell Trainer!"

"That's it," said Pop. "That's it! It don't smell good to me, Breeze."

Johnson was passing. Breeze caught his arm. "Look here, old man, I thought you were going to use a cabin job on this."

Johnson scowled. "Your business is to fly your kite, not to worry about the plane that pulls it."

"Yeah, I know," said Breeze, "but that ship looks new. How come?"

• SKY BIRDS DARE! •

"I borrowed it from a friend of mine," said Johnson in a surly manner.

"Get another or I'm not going," said Breeze, coolly.

"No? Listen, Mister Callahan, I've got your name on this contract, and if you pull out now, I'll sue you out of your last shirt, get me?"

Breeze's fist was closed tight and his eyes were very bleak.

"No," said Pop. "Wait a minute, Breeze. He'll do it. You go on and go through with it and keep your eyes open. That's best."

Johnson pulled away and stalked off toward the power plane. Grauer frowned as he looked after him.

"Look here," said Grauer, in a guttural voice, "What's this all about, eh?"

"Nothing," said Breeze.

"Huh," said Grauer, suspiciously. "I don't want that anything should happen to my *Gretta*."

His *Gretta*, a sailplane of sixty-foot span, was the fond object of all his affection. He went over and caressed the wing, still looking at Johnson.

A few minutes later they were strung out along the field, ready for the takeoff. Breeze, sitting on a borrowed parachute, was last in line.

The O'Dowell Trainer raced its motor and then Johnson waved back, the time-honored signal for "Takeoff!"

Pop stood holding Breeze's wing. "So long."

"See you in Havana," said Breeze. "Tell Patty—"

The power plane began to move. Behind it, on a

two-hundred-foot line, Grauer's sailplane lurched and jerked forward. Behind Grauer, on another two-hundred-foot line, the *Chinook* twitched and then began to trundle forward.

The sailplanes took the air before the power ship and then, its load lightened, the O'Dowell Trainer left the ground. Flying straight ahead, Johnson worked his way upstairs.

It was a weird sight, those two sailplanes following the power ship, like seagulls trailing a liner.

The *Chinook* and the *Gretta*, built to fly at thirty miles, flew themselves at ninety. Breeze sat back and listened to the wind sighing through his struts. The motor far ahead was a small drone in this great bowl of sky.

Breeze reached back and made sure that he had his mail sack. He was to drop off with it at Charleston and land first. In Charleston they would spend the night.

Breeze experienced no great sensation of danger. He had forgotten about the incident that morning and gave himself over to the easy, natural task of piloting his towed ship.

This was not the first time he had been towed by an airplane. But this was the first time he had had another glider ahead of him to watch. But Grauer knew his business and he did it like the well-trained German he was. The *Gretta* flew faultlessly, wings level, never varying from its course.

Seagulls drifting after a liner.

They had not made the mistake of announcing their intention to the world before they started. Pop would be doing that now. Pop would be down in a phone booth saying, "This morning another great stride in aeronautical history and progress. . . ."

It was a weird sight, those two sailplanes following the power ship, like seagulls trailing a liner.

Pop could put it over if he wanted to. Pop knew this game backwards and forwards. And why not? Pop and his kind *were* the game.

Sky train to Havana. There was something thrilling in that. Something thrilling in sitting upstairs and watching the country roll by. Lord, thought Breeze, if he could only make the *Chinook* soar like this.

Virginia was under them. He could see the faint shapes of the Blue Ridge to the west and the low marshy plains to the right. They were two thousand feet up, and the day was as clear as a crystal goblet.

It was good to sit there and feel the rush of air on your face. Good to have a slender, delicate ship under you.

The terrain was changing and they were over rolling, brown plains. Small, weather-beaten shacks were hidden in scraggly trees.

North Carolina already?

Yes. North Carolina. No other place on earth was quite as desolate as this.

Breeze took a drink from a thermos bottle and didn't even notice that the scalding coffee whipped back and smeared his cheek.

Mile after mile they traversed over the highroad of the sky. The sun climbed higher and higher until . . .

Grauer was raising his arm. Breeze looked ahead and down, and there, set between a bay and a river, green with palms and blue with water, was Charleston.

He pulled his rip cord, and the *Chinook* shot up and away

from the train. Breeze nosed her down. He was looking at the airport, making his minute calculations for a glide to a landing. If you overshot in a soaring plane, you had no motor to correct that error.

Singing down through space, hitting an occasional wind bump, Breeze saw the port get bigger and bigger. He did a three-sixty turn and came on in for a perfect landing.

Men rushed out to meet him and then quickly deserted him for Grauer.

Johnson rode earthward on his snorting, sputtering steed, and cameras clicked.

Here they were, with the first leg of the trip done. Breeze gave up his mail sack and the letters which mean so much to stamp collectors.

Now for a good night's sleep and . . .

At nine the next morning they were high in the sky again, sailing southward along the coast, watching the white sand and green underbrush from on high.

Breeze did not feel part of that world down there at all. He knew how an eagle felt sitting on silent wings, a dot in the sky, overlooking the destinies of the world.

Hour after hour and Grauer's perfect flying was still perfect. The Trainer, snarling along as though angry about its burden: the *Gretta*, streaking in level, faultless flight, and then the *Chinook*, flying itself.

Breeze was very satisfied with the world. He thought about Patty. Nothing was wrong with Patty. She just thought gold braid made a man, but she'd get over it. She'd come back when she remembered that gold braid was quickly tarnished and when the Navy bought a couple dozen soaring planes from Breeze.

Sure, Patty was all right.

And then, when Breeze looked down again, Grauer was signaling and pulling his line.

Miami, all white and red and green and blue, was sprawled out under their wings.

Breeze, a little sad about leaving the quiet aloofness of the sky highway, headed down for the port.

Cameras, mail, people, and another night and then . . .

The next morning they were bucking a head wind. It was a hot wind, kicking up tall seas and making the air as rough as the ocean.

It meant very little to Breeze, once they were off. The Trainer could keep plowing ahead, and as the sailplanes were traveling three times as fast as they usually flew, the bumps were no more annoying than small waves are to a fast motorboat. It shook Breeze up a little, but he thought he had nothing to worry about.

The last leg was only two hundred and fifty miles, but three-quarters of it was over water. When they hit the channel between Florida and Cuba the air would be quieter.

Breeze watched Grauer and saw nothing changed. But in this rough air, they could not stay in level line. First one and then another would rise and sink. It required constant attention to keep lines from fouling.

That thin black pencil mark connecting the *Chinook* to the *Greta* was all that kept Breeze in the train. Breeze began to worry about it. The line had been under constant strain for many, many flying hours, and he had a hunch . . .

He looked ahead and saw that they were about to start the crossing. They were flying straight down the coast of Florida and they were already over the Keys. The wind was getting worse.

No place to land there, and if he hit the water, the sailplane wouldn't float an hour. And there were sharks. . . . But why was he worrying? Was it just the water hazard which had gotten him?

He knew then that his hunch was right. About thirty feet from him along the towline, two small tufts of hemp were spinning. He watched them, fascinated. The wind and strain were peeling them back until at last only one strand was there, one thin, weak strand.

Breeze stared down again. Nothing but those small, bleak Keys below, very little beach, a white line of surf. He had to find a place and find it fast.

The *Chinook* gave a terrific lurch and shot upward. Breeze let her go. He needed altitude. The altimeter said two thousand when he leveled out again.

Grauer and the Trainer were cruising onward, growing smaller and smaller against the dazzling sky. They did not seem to realize that Breeze and the *Chinook* were gone. There was something about it which made Breeze smile. He felt like a kid playing hooky.

And then, when he had the *Chinook* cruising its slowest,

he looked down again and knew that any landing he made would be a crash.

No one there if he was hurt. No one to carry the word back. A search would be made when the Trainer landed in Havana, but then it might be too late.

How desolate those Keys looked. No beach, only mounds of sand and bursting spray, kicked upward by the wind.

He could not land there on that curving line of tiny isles. He had to get back to the mainland of Florida somehow.

He banked and headed north. The wind was behind him, and that was some consolation. But the wind would not keep him up. With a twenty-to-one gliding angle he could coast forty thousand feet, or almost eight miles.

But eight miles were nothing in all this lonely expanse of blue channel and brown Keys. Not even a ship in sight, and had there been one, he could not have brought himself to wreck the *Chinook* to save his own neck.

Glider pilots are crazy that way.

He sat upstairs in the great silence and deftly handled the stick. He held her just below stalling point and went down the air like a toboggan.

Death if he crashed in the dunes. Drowning if he hit the sea. Drowning and maybe sharks.

Too bad Patty wasn't here. He'd like to say a word or two to her and tell her he wasn't mad or anything.

Cool wind on his face, good thing it was behind him. It was pretty up here. The whole world was clean and big and colorful. The clouds were piled into gigantic shapes to the east, and the drone of surf came faintly to him from below.

Pretty place to die, anyway.

The Trainer and Grauer were gone. He wondered if they had noticed his absence. If they did, they wouldn't turn back. They knew they could do nothing, not yet. All they could do was remove their helmets at his funeral and . . . that is, if there was a funeral. Up in New England they buried men without having their bodies after the sea had claimed them.

He reached out to the nose of the *Chinook* and pulled in the thirty feet of line which had stayed with him. He coiled it up and looped it over the release ring.

He examined it as well as he could while flying. Yes, he had thought that would be it.

The line had been hacked a little with a knife. So that was it, eh?

Breeze began to get mad. He flew more carefully and looked down and wished he had O'Dowell there with him. He'd drop O'Dowell out and watch him splash, and then circle while the sharks ate him.

But he didn't have O'Dowell. He had the *Chinook,* and about a thousand feet of altitude. The wind was pushing him along, but he would never make the mainland. Those damn Keys . . .

Suddenly he was all soaring pilot.

Wind.

Keys.

To hell with altitude.

Breeze thrust down the *Chinook*'s nose and let the air whistle over his head. He dived straight at the line of surf and then leveled out five hundred feet up. The wings jumped a little as an updraft hit them. He was boosted thirty feet or more.

Breeze relaxed a little. So that was it. Maybe . . .

The wind was a funny thing. Air was not just a chunk of fluid listlessly hovering over the earth. Air was in constant turmoil. When the wind hit a line of trees, it couldn't go through them and it went geysering up, unseen, but still there. And when it went up, it had to come down again, and that made updrafts and downdrafts, the life and soul of soaring.

Then there was the thing called heat lift. On a quiet day, many a power pilot passing over a cornfield was annoyed to feel an air bump pummel him from the underside. The cornfield, being hotter than the surrounding woods, was shooting air upward as smoke shoots out of a sizzling frying pan.

And so it was with these dunes.

All the sea was cool, but the sun made the sand hot and the air rose from them in forceful streams. And the wind hitting the line of surf and the dunes, strengthened the updraft.

It was simple, after that.

All Breeze had to do was sit up there in the *Chinook* and be careful not to go to either side of this constant lift area. The wind, under his wings, supported him. Flying forward at thirty miles an hour and better, he could maintain his original height without any trouble whatever.

Soaring?

Birds have done it since God made birds.

Soaring pilots have done it since sailplanes were first built.

Breeze, flying over those Keys and hot sand dunes, was doing it with a skill and casualness which made power flying a mere, mechanical thing. This took skill, this soaring.

Mile after mile, updraft steadily under him, shoved skywards

GET 4 FREE BOOKS!

You can have the titles in the Stories from the Golden Age delivered to your door by signing up for the book club. Start today, and we'll send you **4 FREE BOOKS** (worth $39.80) as your reward.

―――――◆◇◆―――――

The collection includes 80 volumes (book or audio) by master storyteller L. Ron Hubbard in the genres of science fiction, fantasy, mystery, adventure and western, originally penned for the pulp magazines of the 1930s and '40s.

―――――◆◇◆―――――

YES! ❑

Sign me up for the Stories from the Golden Age Book Club and send me my first book for $9.95 with my **4 FREE BOOKS** (FREE shipping). I will pay only $9.95 each month for the subsequent titles in the series. Shipping is FREE and I can cancel any time I want to.

_____ _____ _____
First Name   Middle Name   Last Name

_____
Address

_____ _____ _____
City   State   ZIP

_____ _____
Telephone   E-mail

Credit/Debit Card #: _____

Card ID# (last 3 or 4 digits): _____ Exp Date: _____/_____

Date (month/day/year) _____/_____/_____

Signature: _____

Comments: _____

Check here ✔ to receive a FREE Stories from the Golden Age catalog or go to: **GoldenAgeStories.com**.

© 2011 Galaxy Press, LLC. All Rights Reserved. Pulp magazines cover artwork are reprinted with permission from Argosy Communications, Inc.; Penny Publications, LLC; Hachette Filipacchi Media; and Condé Nast Publications.

Thank you!

BUSINESS REPLY MAIL
FIRST-CLASS MAIL   PERMIT NO. 75738   LOS ANGELES CA

POSTAGE WILL BE PAID BY ADDRESSEE

GOLDEN AGE BOOK CLUB
GALAXY PRESS
7051 HOLLYWOOD BLVD
LOS ANGELES CA 90028-9771

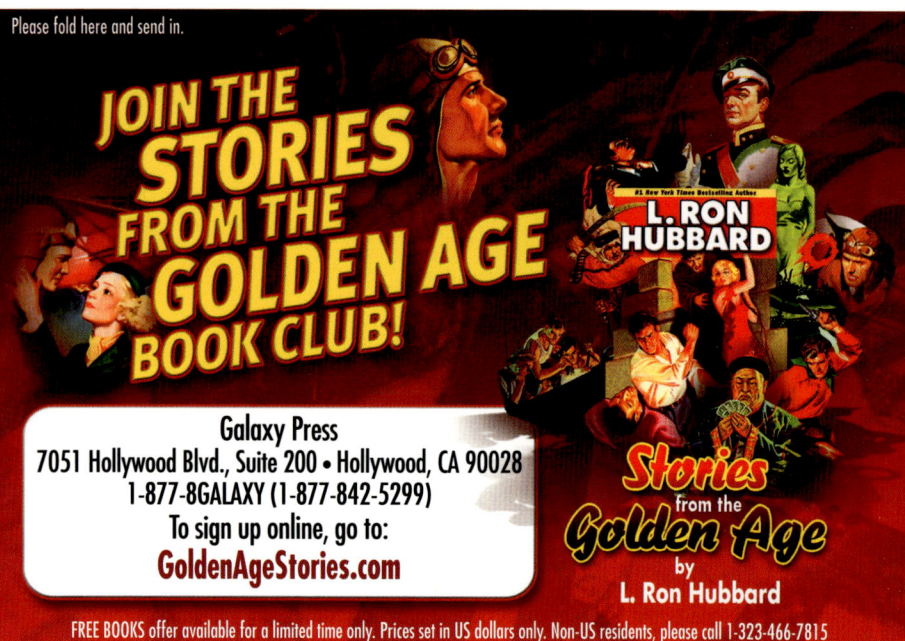

NO POSTAGE
NECESSARY
IF MAILED
IN THE
UNITED STATES

Please fold here and send in.

JOIN THE STORIES FROM THE GOLDEN AGE BOOK CLUB!

Galaxy Press
7051 Hollywood Blvd., Suite 200 • Hollywood, CA 90028
1-877-8GALAXY (1-877-842-5299)
To sign up online, go to:
GoldenAgeStories.com

Stories from the Golden Age
by L. Ron Hubbard

FREE BOOKS offer available for a limited time only. Prices set in US dollars only. Non-US residents, please call 1-323-466-7815 for pricing information or go to GoldenAgeStories.com. Sales tax where applicable. Terms, prices and conditions subject to change. Subscription subject to acceptance. You may cancel your subscription at any time. Galaxy Press reserves the right to reject any order or cancel any subscription. If under 18, a parent or guardian must sign.

faster than he could coast landwards, he was making for the mainland with a sure hand.

Mile after mile, Breeze sat back and enjoyed himself. To hell with sharks and crashes. He was in his element. He was the sailing ship of the sky and even the frigate birds which skimmed along with him, staring at him with beady eyes and wondering what right this thing had taking up their especial function and their special air, were moved to awed admiration.

Delicate fingers, a sure sense of balance, and an eye which could almost see that invisible uprush of air he rode, Breeze had everything he wanted in life, except Patty.

Not much later he sighted a white beach ahead of him. It was a broad beach, long and smooth, just the place for a landing. That was the mainland. Some houses were there and some fishermen were caulking a boat, and the world was very peaceful.

A great shadow swept down the sand, coming as silently as a ghost. The fishermen leaped up and stared. One of them yelled and ran toward a boathouse in fear.

Breeze skimmed in for a landing and stepped out on the sand, looking altogether too satisfied for a man who had just cheated death.

They listened to him, those fishermen, and although they failed to understand just how a man could ride the wind without a motor, they made him welcome.

Pop found him there four days afterwards. Pop was glad to see him, but Pop looked somewhat bedraggled and harassed.

"Look," said Pop, even before he had gotten out of the battered tow car. "Look!"

Breeze read the papers Pop gave him, and then he too felt bad about it.

"Read it." cried Pop. "That guy O'Dowell promoted this flight to show what his Trainer could do, and there you don't see anything but pictures of that damned Trainer. What a fine ship it is to pull such a load, and all that. And it don't say anything about you, except that you tried to wreck the flight by refusing to go on from Miami."

Pop gripped the newspapers as though he would have liked to strangle them. "Damn, damn, damn that guy O'Dowell."

Breeze gave him a crooked smile. "To hell with it, Pop, we'll think up something else. Listen, I've been figuring something out for several days here, and you know what I think? I think I can start up in Pennsylvania and soar right down the Appalachians to southern West Virginia. How about that, Pop? Don't you think that would stand them on their ear?"

Breeze had advanced it to cheer Pop up. It did. Pop pointed to the trailer behind the car.

"Get that sailplane on there, Breeze. Let's go and make this guy O'Dowell look like a monkey-faced baboon."

CHAPTER SIX

Breeze Welcomes Storm

IN the days of wooden ships—and iron men—sea captains reputedly had noses which could smell out all manner of weather. In fact, these old windjammer captains could often outguess a weather station in spite of the odds of instruments. Whether a sailing ship lay becalmed or moved depended solely upon the wind—and the captain's eye for weather.

Breeze Callahan, standing there silhouetted against the murky blue sky, did not look like a sailing captain, but there was a certain calculating squint to his blue eyes and a certain angle of his head which made it seem that he smelled the wind for tidings of what it would bring.

On the ridge beside him was the *Chinook,* its wings quiet as though it rested and waited with anticipation.

Breeze looked down the smoky hills, across the rolling mountains of Pennsylvania, and liked the taste of the air.

"Storm," said Breeze, with the utmost satisfaction.

He had been waiting three days now, standing there on that ridge, waiting for a storm. He needed a storm. He would have to have one. And his meteorology—or perhaps a sixth sense—told him that an abrupt summer thundershower was near at hand. Somewhere down the slope a tree frog was croaking, and that, too meant storm.

Pop was nervous, but he was smiling. During the last few

weeks some of Pop's optimism had melted down, bursting out only when Breeze needed heartening. Now that a storm was coming, Pop felt a sense of imminent loss. Soon Breeze would sail up against a murky sky and leave Pop alone there on that ridge. Alone in the rushing wind.

Breeze looked to the north. The sky was darkening there. Breeze lifted his chin a little to feel the crisp caress of the coming gale. The *Chinook* shifted restlessly as though anxious to be up and away.

A drumming roar was in the sky, echoing against the hills. Into the quiet sailed a gray monster of the skyways, a transport plane.

Breeze watched it idly. He had nothing in common with a transport plane. He had no liking for the grinding engines which tugged metal and men hastily across the blasted heavens.

A long field, covered with close cropped grass, sprawled out at the base of the slope, plenty of room for a landing power ship. But Breeze did not think . . .

The gray monster swooped down, motors suddenly mute, singing through the air as it coasted in for a landing. The crump, crump, crump of the bouncing wheels came up to the pair on the crest.

"Why, it's a Navy plane!" said Breeze, startled.

Pop blinked at the outspread wings below them. The cabin had opened to emit four people and one of them a woman.

"Patty!" Pop yelled.

Breeze raced down the hillside to meet the up-toiling

group. He slid to a dusty stop before the girl and beamed at her. "Hello, Patty."

"Hello, Breeze," she said, laughing. "Look what I brought you!"

Breeze looked at them. Captain Daniels and Lieutenants Sweeney and Maynard.

"Harumph," said Daniels. "*Cough* ... harrumph." He paused halfway up and panted awhile. "Young man ... harrumph ... this young lady of yours is a most pleasant young person but ... *pant, pant*, harrumph ... but damnably insistent."

Sweeney looked suspiciously at Breeze and then Patty. Maynard looked at Sweeney.

Captain Daniels removed his cap and pawed at his gray hair. "We got word from the weather stations up north, young man, that there's a terrific storm coming down this way, following the ridge, so to speak. You'd better get that plaything back on the trailer and go home."

"A storm?" said Breeze in elation. He turned to Pop. "There! See, I told you a storm was coming. Say, that's swell of you fellows to come all the way up from Washington just to tell me that."

The three officers were staring at him as though they questioned his sanity.

"Harumph ..." began Daniels. "Perhaps you didn't hear me, young man. I said there was a storm coming down this way. A lightning storm."

"But that's fine!" cried Breeze, waving his arms to the north. "Can't you see? A storm! That's swell!"

They had reached the top by this time and Daniels sat down on a rock. The lieutenants stood on either side of Patty as though ready to protect her against the madman they had found here.

"Say, are you nuts?" said Maynard to Breeze. "This girl came storming into Anacostia wailing about you being up here out of communication and she said there was a storm sailing right down at you and we'd have to do something about it. And you . . ."

Patty smiled wickedly and thrust her small hands into the pockets of her borrowed trench coat with the air of utmost satisfaction. The three officers stared at her.

"Hmmmmmm," said Daniels. "Young lady, something tells me that you were pulling an act. This young man isn't worried a bit."

"Worried?" said Breeze. "I'm tickled to death. Why," he said in sudden amazement, "how did you think I'd soar down this ridge for a distance record if I didn't have a storm pushing me along, huh? For God's sakes, I mean . . . Why, I want to make it three hundred miles if I can. They'd gone almost two hundred in Germany, and I want to beat that."

Sweeney growled something which sounded like a curse, and Maynard said, "Look here, young fellow, whether you know it or not, even a power plane would get a hell of a licking in a storm like this one that's coming. I appreciate the fact that you want to do something, but believe me, it's no use. You haven't got a chance."

"You ever soar?" said Breeze, innocently.

Maynard scowled again. "Why . . . er . . . of course not.

What fool would pay any attention to soaring when he could get in a plane which had a good fast engine on the nose, eh? Well, well, of course not. You see what I mean? Of course, it might be all right if you didn't have money enough to buy the engine, but after all . . ."

Daniels interrupted him. "See there, the north's getting darker by the second. We've got to get out of here, gentlemen. Miss Donegan, are you coming with us?"

Patty looked at Breeze and then at the frail *Chinook*. She felt the jerky blasts of the wind rolling up over the crest and suddenly she was afraid.

"Breeze . . . Breeze, do you have to try it now? Can't you wait . . ."

Breeze was puzzled. He could not realize that they were afraid of this coming blow, that it meant so little to them that he was about to try for an international distance record in a motorless plane. He stood there with the wind tugging at his jacket as though the wind urged him to come along upstairs and play.

"Please," said Patty, with a scared glance at the lowering clouds which were beginning to roll higher and higher above the smoky hills. Scuds sent their shadows racing along the ground and the sun blinked off and on like a warning beacon.

Breeze stepped back, away from them as though they were trying to hurt him.

"Look here," said Daniels, "you fold up that plaything, Callahan. If you want to fly, I'll have you made a Naval cadet, but leave this sort of thing for madmen. Don't be a kid, Callahan. Don't scare this young lady out of her wits. She thought it was mighty fine of you and she argued for an hour to get us to go this morning, and you owe her better than you're giving."

Sweeney said, "Aw, let him go."

Maynard looked down at the transport plane. He was getting nervous. The wind was coming up and getting cold, and he knew they had to get out of there before hell broke about them. He looked back from that sturdy giant to the flimsy, thin wings of the *Chinook* and grunted at the contrast.

"Kid stuff," Maynard said. "Pull it apart, Callahan, before the wind blows it away."

"Please," begged Patty. She knew that Breeze needed a storm, but this . . .

Breeze lifted the *Chinook*'s hood and slid into the pit. He buckled his safety belt and glanced to the north. The wind was calling and he had to go.

Pop said, "Take hold of these wings, will you?"

Daniels stood up and took one, shaking his head sadly.

Patty thrust her hands deeper and deeper into the trench coat pockets. The wind was pressing the skirts against her slim body and rumpling her hair.

"Breeze!" she cried, running to the cockpit. "Breeze! Don't go! Listen, Breeze . . ."

"So long, Patty," grinned Breeze. He touched her hand and gently put it away from the hood.

The ridge was flat, a good runway for the car. Pop clenched the scarred steering wheel, looked back and caught Breeze's signal. Pop put the car in gear, and then the towrope stretched and jerked taut.

The *Chinook*'s wings, leveling out, shivered in the violence of the wind. Breeze fought the stick and rudders for a moment, straightening out. The car was going faster and faster. The *Chinook* sang and whispered with eagerness and leaped off and up, buffeted by the rough air.

Those on the ground saw sunlight gleaming through the thin wings and looked upward with strained faces. They heard the faint crack as Breeze released the rope. The rope came straggling down out of the blue and gray sky to coil itself in endless loops upon the slope.

The sailplane swerved in a wide bank, jumping under the hammer blows of vicious updrafts. They could see small movements as Breeze eased the stick back and forth, keeping level, seeking the rise.

"Damned fool." said Daniels, disgruntled.

"Serves him right," echoed Sweeney.

"No sense to it," complained Maynard, "when you can have a nice fast motor up there in the nose hauling you along."

Patty didn't dare to breathe. She was watching the sailplane as it flashed down the ridge, disappearing gradually into the south.

The strong wind was howling now, pressing the trench coat against her back as though urging her to follow, as though bidding her to take the sky roads with Breeze.

The Chinook *sang and whispered with eagerness and leaped off and up, buffeted by the rough air.*

CHAPTER SEVEN

While Storm Devils Dance

BREEZE CALLAHAN wanted plenty of sky room and he could have all there was with this wind. He had a gale behind him and he had an endless ridge which extended all the way across Pennsylvania, Maryland and West Virginia.

Hitting that ridge, the baffled wind shot almost straight up in a continuous, unvarying stream. Five hundred feet over the rocky hogback Breeze was having very little trouble staying aloft.

It was one of those days sail pilots pray for and rarely get. He was far enough ahead of the storm to miss the whirling turbulence, but if he lost the long updraft, he could always fall back upon the nearest greasy black scud cloud for more power.

The wind comes out of the bottom of scud clouds, curls forward and up, and any skillful sail pilot can ride there, pushed along and held up by the wind itself.

To Breeze, this was all for his benefit. God had spread out the murky world especially for his pleasure. God had given him this storm for wings such as his.

In his sighing, rocking, buffeted ship, Breeze was grinning. Rough seas always entice the sailor, rough air always dares the soaring pilot.

No motor here to mar the scene. Nothing but wind and the

whisper of wings. Man against the elements in direct, powerful conflict. Breeze looked upon power craft as something to be flown by unimaginative men who admitted their lack of strength. In his enthusiasm he saw no impracticability to soaring. He saw only the glamor of the battle against the skies.

Old sailing ship men hated the smug aloofness of the steamer. A man did not have to hope and fight when he had thousands of horses in his hold to pull him through the seas. Old sailing ship men prayed in the calm and cursed in the tempests, but, shaggy and coarse though they were, they thrilled to the scream of wind through their canvas and grinned with delight and ecstasy when their leeward rail went down and the bows began to streak across the tumbling green sea.

Engines.

Who wants to be a slave to engines, when the sky is free and wings are strong and the red gods of danger are calling?

Who would debase himself with a throttle when wind is roaring upwards and when black storm rushes down to tromp and stumble on your flying heels?

Whispering struts and sighing wings, buffeted and shaken by blast after blast. Breeze rode his silent steed, all alone against the murky sky, far above the outspread world, which could only crouch down and shiver under the approaching storm.

The ship was as sensitive as an Arabian thoroughbred, answering to the slightest touch, quivering and fleet, proud and graceful. Breeze swooped down the skies, glancing back from time to time and laughing at the storm which tried to catch him.

Great piles of sullen murk were charging after him. Regiment after regiment following the greedy van, shot through by long lances of lightning, while the earth shook beneath the savage onslaught.

Rising and falling, whipping and shivering, the sailplane headed south.

Breeze flew with deft, quick fingers. His watchful eyes saw each change in contour below him. Every slope meant another shift of the updraft, and with that uncanny skill with which birds are born and which men have to acquire, Breeze knew almost to a foot where he would find the maximum lift.

The baffled wind, shooting forward, striking cliffs and geysering upward, threw him skyward like a chip.

Power. Who cared for puny horses? Who cared for clanking steel? Who would drop so low as to breathe the stench of gas fumes, when wind and sky were free and wild?

Breeze was at a thousand. Even here the updraft was strong enough to shake the teeth of a power plane. The wind was swifter now. Forty-mile wind and racing scud clouds thrust him forward and onward.

He was dropping back toward the storm, but he did not care. As long as he could keep from being sucked into the violence of those greasy piles of rain and mist he was safe enough.

The only sound he could hear above the shrill song of his wings was the occasional mutter of thunder behind him. Thunder could not hurt him. Those jagged yellow swords stabbing outwards from the masses could not touch him. He was too fast for them.

The country below him became more and more broken. Mountains, with their tops swathed in cotton, stood up on all sides. He stayed with the ridge and rushed onward, sun on his wings, rain and tempest behind him, his shadow whisking over the earth as though hard put to keep pace with him.

His arms were growing weary with the constant strain, but he neither noticed nor cared for that. He could fly until his arms refused to move and still, somehow, he could go on.

It would be much harder to stop than to continue. Much harder.

Breeze looked back and laughed again. As if that stumbling, clumsy storm could catch him now.

He was not aware of passing time until, when he was thrown sideways for an instant, sun flashed from the altimeter. It startled him because he had thought the sun was still on his left. But it was on his right, low on the horizon to the west.

Late afternoon.

He had been sitting there flying hour after hour, racing air mile after air mile. He had flown all through the day, six hours and more and now it would soon be dark.

The storm was still pursuing him, having come a little nearer now. He realized that to land would be to hand himself over to the violence he had so long mocked.

But he had to land. His arms were numb and his reactions were slow. He was not staying as level as he might, and he was not as careful of his lift. Twice now he had hit downdrafts which had slammed him hundreds of feet toward the ground before he could recover.

And as he looked back another downdraft hit him.

The bottom fell out. The sudden blow from above forced him into a steep dive. Valiantly he gathered speed, leveled out and raced for another lift area before he lost all his altitude.

Wind hit him from every direction, pummeling him, rocking him until his head whirled.

Rain spattered on his right wing. He looked up into a lowering mass of greasy cotton.

The storm, denied so long, had him.

Lightning ripped by, almost splitting his eardrums. The sailplane veered, yawing and shivering. The controls jerked and fought his irksome hand.

Everything went black about him, and then lightning made the wings shimmer for a brief moment. Rain washed him and cut his cheeks.

The *Chinook* reeled as though in agony. The wings fluttered under the strain of crosscurrents and the mailed fists of weather.

Left wing down, he was diving. He hit an updraft and skyrocketed, right wing down, wind on his cheek. He was slipping like a sword slashed sideways.

Level and diving again. Up with his nose, pointing straight at yellow snake tongues which lanced him.

In a matter of seconds he was drenched.

He knew now how tired he was. He could not make his arms move quickly enough. He was slow, slow, and he couldn't see.

Somewhere below were the mountains which had claimed so many power pilots. He had to land down there, had to land in rain and thunder and darkness and save the *Chinook*. He had to do that. He had to find a place where these frail wings would be sheltered through the night. He himself could stand the wind, but not his wings.

He saw the labyrinths of mist all about him in the next lightning flash. His ears were shaken by the rumbling, whipping blast which followed instantly. That had been close.

He was in some mighty cavern filled with demons. He was staring at ugly, misshapen heads and lashing dragon tails.

The storm had him now and the jaws were snapping shut. How long could these frail wings stand this beating?

Updraft again. Vicious whistling air blasted him skyward through the blackness. He fought to hold it. If he could get up . . . Puny wings now. Small, thin wings. Hauled and torn and wrenched, dripping with rain which came in blinding gray sheets. Cymbals and drums went mad through the abruptly lighted heavens.

Up and still up again. There were mountains here at hand. Where were those sullen, drenched slopes? Were they waiting for the crunched remains of those silver, frail wings?

Up, and still up. Hope struggled valiantly to warm him. His mouth was set in a hard, fighting line. This was a battle worthy of him and his strength. If he had ever worried about his stamina and coolness, he was at ease about it now.

Up again in a blasting, rocketing dash, higher into the storm.

And then the thunder was behind him. This was a line squall. The main command of the greasy legions were still somewhere behind him. That small, round mass had lately been his prison. Lightning still shot through it as though angry to have lost him.

He caught another lift area and rode it wearily. He had to stay ahead, and get even farther ahead. He had to find a piece of level ground and land before it was dark. He could not fight this all night. He had come far enough now. He had beaten any existing record. He knew that. He had come two hundred miles and more. Two hundred miles without an engine ahead of a storm which made power men cower before its fury.

And now he had to land in this piled up country.

Far to the right, like some block left on the floor by a careless child, he saw the house. There was a field close at hand, a barn set farther back. He could find shelter there, shelter and warmth and food. He could protect these silver wings before the storm overrode him again.

He put the nose down and ran for it. Wind shrilled by as he quickened his speed. The field grew larger and larger. He circled to gauge his distance better and then sailed in and settled on the rough earth.

He did not brake. He let his ship trundle up against the wind with its excess speed until he was almost upon the house. A man in a ragged suit of jeans came running toward him, mouth open, eyes staring in surprise.

The man had never seen a power ship back here in these West Virginia hills, much less a soaring plane. The goggled face in the cockpit frightened him.

Breeze shoved back the hood and stepped out, thrusting off his helmet. "Here, pick up that wing there. Fast now, it's raining already. Is there anything in your barn?"

"I . . . I reckon not. The gov'mint . . ."

"Faster man, I'll guide it! Run!"

They skimmed the *Chinook* across the barnyard to the narrow door.

"Pliers," cried Breeze. "Get me some pliers quick!"

With them, he removed the wings with all speed. It was raining hard now, and the evening sky was sullen and black. Thunder was rolling across the valley.

Breeze thrust the *Chinook* into the barn and closed the doors upon it, breathing easier now that that was done. He was about to ask for something to drink when the thunder became steady and louder.

Breeze stared up at the heavens in amazement.

The transport plane was landing on the field.

CHAPTER EIGHT

A Sail Pilot Masters Power

PATTY threw herself out of the cabin and into Breeze's arms. "Oh, Breeze, I've been frantic! Are you all right? You poor dear, you look worn-out."

"But how . . . ?" said Breeze.

"We followed you, damn it!" roared Captain Daniels. "She . . . She made us follow you. We're almost out of gas and we've got to get the hell out of here before the storm wrecks this plane. Think I want to be checked on pay the rest of my life just because you pull something foolish like this distance stunt?"

Breeze looked at the man quickly and then saw with sinking heart that Captain Daniels was not in the least impressed by the fact that a motorless plane could be so skillfully handled that it could traverse more than two hundred miles of mountainous country.

"You didn't have to follow me," said Breeze, stiffly.

"She made us!" roared Daniels.

The lanky West Virginian stood aside, too amazed to speak or move. Nothing like this had ever happened in his mountains before.

Sweeney swarmed down on the man. "Look here! Have you got gasoline? See, here's money. We've got to have gasoline and fast before this storm hits us. We'll be overdue at Washington. Get us gas, do you hear?"

The West Virginian stared at the money and pocketed it. He shuffled off with Maynard and Sweeney bearing down upon him, and showed them two rusty drums where he kept tractor and car fuel.

While they gassed up, Captain Daniels was glaring at the thunderheads, which came nearer and nearer through the flurries of rain, and muttered between his teeth.

"Damned young upstart. Get us into this mess, would he."

Sweeney and Maynard, spattered with the cheap gas, finished the refueling and climbed into the ship. Breeze was startled to see Pop there. Pop was sitting very quietly, as though a bolt of lightning had hit him.

"They cussed all day, son," said Pop, and then in a burst of optimism, "but when they get to thinking it over, they'll see what you did. It was swell, son. Swell! Never saw anything so grand in all my life."

"Let's get the hell out of here," snorted Daniels.

Breeze gave some orders about his *Chinook* to the West Virginian and then the transport plane roared, all three motors snarling, down the field and into the air.

The wind was bumpy and in this monster each updraft and downdraft was merely an annoying incident. Sweeney was at the controls, flying with a heavy fist on wheel and throttles.

"We'll climb over it!" Sweeney yelled back.

Daniels grunted and gave Breeze a glare. "We wouldn't have gotten into this if you'd listened to us. Now we'll have to land in the dark and make all sorts of cockeyed explanations of why we're overdue. Young man, the Navy has something to do besides follow crackbrained kids."

Breeze returned the glare and then sat back. Patty was looking up into his face and he was glad of that. It was hard to talk in the cabin, the motors made such a racket.

This was bullying, angry flight. Nothing thrilling about it, just a means of traveling from one point to another in the minimum time.

Breeze was weary and Patty's presence was soothing to his tired nerves. He leaned back heavily and felt her hair rippling against his cheek. He closed his eyes and then . . .

He could not have been asleep for more than fifteen minutes, but something had changed. This lunging demon was lunging no more. Only one engine was keeping up. Breeze started up and saw that Daniels was white and Sweeney was crouched over the wheel in tense expectancy.

"Go back!" yelled Daniels.

"It's closed in back there!" cried Sweeney.

Breeze looked through the spattered glass of the window and saw the murk below them. They were high, very high, but they were still in the storm. Evening was fading into blackness.

"Won't it fly with one engine?" cried Breeze.

"Hell no!" roared Daniels. "It's that damned gas! There was water in it and the wing engines—"

Breeze was half on his feet. Patty and Pop tried to pull him back. He tossed them aside.

"You mean," said Breeze in Daniels' ear, "you mean you're going to commit suicide by landing in this murk? There's nothing but mountains down there. You'll kill us all."

"I'm in command here!" bellowed Daniels.

"The hell you are!" said Breeze. "Get out of my way!"

"Sit down, you pup!"

"Get out of my way!"

"By God," screamed Maynard, "I'll throw you over the side if you don't sit still."

"Yeah?" said Breeze.

Maynard struggled up. The cabin was too low for Breeze to stand, but he reached over Daniels and grabbed Maynard by the shirt front.

Bodily he slammed Maynard down into a seat and then thrust off Daniels' clinging hands.

"He's gone nuts!" Sweeney yelled. "He'll wreck us! Don't let him get up here!"

Breeze stepped around Daniels, balancing himself in the lurching cabin.

"Get away from that wheel," snapped Breeze.

"Get back!" cried Sweeney.

Breeze gripped the lieutenant by the collar and hauled him out of the pilot's seat. The transport plane flew itself for the next few seconds.

Breeze slammed Sweeney back into the cabin. A Very pistol was in its holster under the throttles. Breeze picked it up and thrust it at Pop.

"Give them a dose of signal lights if they move," yelled Breeze.

He slid in under the wheel and looked intently at the panel. The mute faces of the instruments told him very little. He did not know nor care about such mechanical, fancy things. All he wanted was an altimeter and a compass. These were all right.

He glanced back and saw that the officers were watching him with white, strained faces. They had lost altitude in that last scramble, and now anything done to recover the controls would mean a crash. They could only sit there and watch.

Breeze juggled the wheel, pulled it to him and pushed it away and was finally satisfied with it. Wasn't a bad control system, he thought, but sort of bulky. He had never flown anything like this.

"He'll wreck us," said Daniels, hoarsely. "That motor won't carry us and we'll hit a mountainside . . ."

Breeze was headed south. In the dying light a great scud cloud was outlined. It came sharply to them when the lightning flashed.

Breeze deliberately headed down. The one motor would help quite a little, but it couldn't do it all. That scud was just the thing to keep them going.

He descended upon it, and although he could no longer see it very well, occasional, ripping blasts of lightning oriented it for him again.

The storm was helping now.

The wings were suddenly bolstered. The altimeter needle trembled and began to come up. They were holding their own now, even climbing a little.

The crying wind was coming out from under that cloud

and curling up over the leading edge of it. That was all Breeze needed. He nursed the engine's throttle and cruised back and forth.

The altimeter climbed steadily and then there was no more lift there.

Lightning crashed and another ugly thunderhead loomed to their right.

Again the transport plane's nose went down and the mighty monster shuddered as it struck the vicious updraft of shrieking wind.

Up again. Steadily, surely, relentlessly up. The altimeter registered two thousand and was still climbing. It was growing cold. The black squares of windows in the cabin sparked as the lightning flared.

In those brief instants of light they could see Breeze. He looked bigger than he had before. He looked bigger than the whole cabin. Behind him, Daniels was staring with disbelief.

Breeze had forgotten that those others were there. He had the storm about him, and he was using the violence of the storm to carry on.

Forced landings in these hills had been tried before. Always something had happened. There were no fields. Transport ships, commercial ships, private craft, all met the same fate when they came down.

The mountains were strewn with the bones of dead ships.

And Breeze carried on. The altimeter trembled up to three thousand feet, and still the storm was over them. He traveled through a fantastic world of black corridors, towering castles and blasting greenish light. The sound of the engine was muffled and made puny by thunder.

And still they flew.

The compass no longer said south. It had drifted toward the west a little. No one knew where they were, much less Breeze. He was only concerned with staying aloft until they could land in safety.

There were airports and beacons somewhere along here. Perhaps, through these stacked masses of blackness, he could see them and pick them out.

He remembered after a while that there were radio beacons, but he could not use them.

From cloud tip to cloud, deeper into the storm, he made the transport fly. He had magic in his fingers. The altimeter held its contest with him and lost.

This was just a local storm. It could not spread over the whole eastern seaboard. Somewhere, somehow, he would find a way out.

Meantime, they were still in the air.

Abruptly, the windows turned a milky white. The moon was shining over the storm. A placid moon, untroubled by violence and the small strivings of men.

Breeze grinned at it. He still had lift along the edge of this storm, and he was using it. The one engine was driving along, taking some of the burden.

And though it appeared to those in the ship that this must certainly come to an end, and though they knew that the nightmare had not begun, they began to watch Breeze and the moon. The two went together somehow. Both above the storm and earthly things.

The lift kept up and when it did fail, Breeze found it again. Cloud soaring by moonlight was a stunt that had been done before. The Germans . . .

An eye was winking at them from the ground. It was a very small thing. It was white and then red, red, red and then white. Beyond it was another and another and then a whole blur of white. Aviation beacons and . . . Knoxville, Tennessee!

The world was calm beneath the blue white rays. Cars were running along a road, sending out banners of light before them. The storm was rumbling along on its own cloud highway. The one engine was stretching their glide and they were high enough to make that square of color, the airport.

"Take this thing, will you?" said Breeze. "I don't think I can land it."

Sweeney slid silently into the pilot's seat and switched on their landing lights. He brought the ship down to earth without a word.

Breeze was weary. He stumbled out of the cabin and leaned against a jury strut, trying to get some feeling into his legs and arms.

Oh, he'd done it now, he thought. They'd be very mad indeed when they had to spend the night in Knoxville all because of him. And he'd been pretty nasty back there. He'd browbeaten them into letting him . . .

"Breeze," said Patty softly. "Breeze, that was wonderful."

Captain Daniels said, "Harumph! Cough, cough! Young

• SKY BIRDS DARE! •

man, you've been holding out on me. How many thousand hours have you put in on power ships?"

"I never flew one before tonight, sir. I've always flown sailplanes."

"That's right," said Pop, proudly. "I never could get him to fly anything but sailplanes."

Sweeney looked at Maynard, and Maynard looked at Daniels. Sudden respect was in their eyes, but something hopeless, too, as they realized that Patty had just played them along to help Breeze.

"Young man," said Captain Daniels, "I owe you an apology. I never thought soaring could mean anything to power flight. I never thought there was anything new to learn in flying at all. I thought we had covered it.

"Well, Mr. Callahan," he continued, "I think you've proved your point tonight. We're amateurs, all of us, compared to you. I . . . er . . . I had an appointment with a fellow named O'Dowell for tomorrow morning, but I realize something now. This young lady of yours told me something about him but I wouldn't believe her. Now I know she's right. You were saying something a few months back about selling the Navy a lot of your soaring planes. I think I can arrange that. In fact, Mr. Callahan, I know that I can. And we'll get you to teach us to use them, too."

Pop Donegan drew him away. Pop knew all about it. Pop said, "Yep, we'll be able to turn out some good Navy pilots for you now. Turn 'em out on gliders, and then graduate them into power stuff when they know all about air and such. Yessir, Captain, we'll turn out some real ones."

Pop was looking straight at Sweeney when he said it. Sweeney grinned at him and slapped him on the back. Maynard looked over at the dark patch under the wing. He was grinning, too.

"Hey, Mr. Callahan," said Captain Daniels, "I know you love her and I know that not even a pilot like you is worthy of her. But dammit, man, let's all get a cab uptown and find something to eat. We've got a celebration to take care of."

Patty towed weary Breeze toward the waiting cab. Patty was walking proudly.

Story Preview

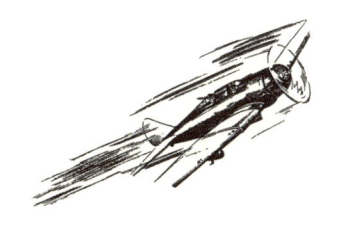

Story Preview

NOW that you've just ventured through one of the captivating tales in the Stories from the Golden Age collection by L. Ron Hubbard, turn the page and enjoy a preview of *Trouble on His Wings*. Join Johnny Brice, a hard-working "picture-chaser" and top-dog reporter—until he meets the pretty Jinx, and things just keep going wrong.

Trouble on His Wings

TOSSED to the crest and let down like a roller coaster into the trough, he could not see what was happening, save for the growing bulk of the steamer. Was it going to run him down? For the matchstick thing it had appeared from the air, it certainly was increased in size. Johnny hadn't ever seen anything so big.

He was growing tired, and the chill was eating through him like knives. Wouldn't the fools ever get busy? Were they going to let a guy drown?

Suddenly a boat hook fixed on his collar, choking him. He was towed to the gunwale of the lifeboat and sailors snatched him over the edge, to drop him in the bottom, like a floundering cod.

"Okay," said the mate, standing at the tiller. "Prepare to give way. Give way all together! Stroke!"

Johnny sighed with relief and watched the brawny sailors heave-ho on their oars, sending the lifeboat on its crazy, tipsy journey back to the side of the drifting steamer. Johnny grinned a little to himself. It wasn't everybody that could stop a ship like that.

Tackles were hooked into the boat fore and aft, and blocks creaked as they were lifted up the palisade of rusty steel toward the boat deck. The davits swung, first one, then the other, and the lifeboat was over the side and back into its cradle.

A thunderously scowling man wearing tarnished braid, fastened upon Johnny. "What's the idea? I thought your ship was coming down, but it's flown off by itself! Is this some new kind of a ———, ———, ———, ——— stunt?"

"Johnny Brice, of World News. Get your picture in all the theaters, Captain—"

"News! Why, you young—"

"Ah, ah!" warned Johnny. "Ladies present, Captain." And he slid out of the irate mariner's grasp and through the crowd.

As he went, a young lady suddenly backed out of the crowd and appeared to be on her way into a passage. The movement attracted Johnny's eye and the girl looked as though she was unhappy to be noticed. Johnny decided that it might be shock from the wreck. She was too beautiful to be swimming around in the ocean and scorched by flame.

"World News," said Johnny. "We bought some pictures by radio. Whoever's got 'em, trot 'em out." He spoke to the crowd but he noted that the girl was more uneasy than before, though reluctant to retreat. Her wide blue eyes were almost frightened, strange in their intensity upon him.

Several passengers ran to get their salvaged films. There were plenty of rolls, thanks to the penchant of tourists for movie cameras.

"Sight unseen," said Johnny. "Five hundred dollars a roll."

A little fat man wearing nothing much more than a blanket, but gripping his precious film, stared at Johnny with disbelief. "You won't even have to see if it shows in the pictures?"

"Somebody was bound to get some," said Johnny. "Come on, the rest of you. Shell out." He took his checkbook in hand and started to write.

Ten minutes later he had spent three thousand dollars of company money and had a questionable batch of film rolled up in his rubber bag.

"You're a fool," snapped the captain, still peeved. "You could have bought all this when we docked. You won't get it there any sooner."

"Oh, won't I?" grinned Johnny. "Collect from the company for the delay. World News pays for its exclusives."

The amphib was hovering in the sky and Johnny turned to the passengers. Again he noticed that the girl shrank back, though her appearance and not her conduct made the bigger impression upon him. In this mob of out-of-shape men and variously misbuilt tourist women, all in blankets or borrowed sailor clothes, the girl was the only one whose poise was not shattered by exterior appearance.

Johnny moved over to the rail, taking the captain with him. "Have you got a Mrs. Felznick aboard? A sort of lumpy old dame, I think. She'd have her hands full of jewels if she drowned, unless she let go."

The captain had melted ever so little under the persuasive smile of the young man. It was said in the business, that Johnny could talk and grin his way through the place to which all newsreel cameramen probably go. Calling an officer of the ill-fated *Kalolo*, the captain put the question.

The man, singed and chagrined at the loss of his ship, shook his head impatiently. "Just finished compiling the list.

We haven't any such name aboard this ship—and we haven't our passenger list, though there's a duplicate in the company office. I seem to remember the name, but—" he swallowed hard. The loss of passengers was too heavy upon him, "But I guess she must have been among the dead."

"The old man is going to take this hard," muttered Johnny. "Thanks, Skipper, for the lift."

"Huh?" said the captain.

Johnny had acted before anyone else realized what he was doing. He went over the rail in a long, clean dive, far out from the ship, so as to miss the propellers—if he could. He came up and saw the side terrifyingly close to him. He struck out as fast as he could, rubber container clutched against his side. The steamer swirled on past to leave Johnny floundering and half-drowned in the boiling wake. He fought to keep afloat, spluttering and coughing. The world was a tangle of green mountains, snowcapped with froth, and all the peaks were falling in upon him. He turned about wildly to locate Irish and found that he faced the stern of the slowing steamer. And as he looked he saw a white figure perch on the rail and soar seaward, straight into the propeller boil. He had no time to speculate on the identity of the mad diver, he was too occupied with the possibility that he would be keeping company, in a moment, with a chewed-up corpse.

"And me without a camera!" he swore.

The steamer had stopped its way for a moment, but now, with a sizzling sea curse the captain rang for headway and the SS *Birmingham Alabama* departed from Johnny's life, just as abruptly as all things parted from a man in such an unstable career.

He heard an engine barking and bellowing as a cunning hand worked the throttle to keep the nose into the waves. A wing was a few feet from Johnny and he thankfully struggled toward it. As it dipped, he grasped it to be pulled bodily out of the sea with the ship's next lurch. Ducked twice, he finally made the catwalk to find Irish wildly pointing to starboard.

"What's the matter?" shouted Johnny. And then he needed no answer. Somebody was swimming strongly toward them and Johnny understood that the propellers had been cheated of a meal.

To find out more about *Trouble on His Wings* and how you can obtain your copy, go to www.goldenagestories.com.

Glossary

STORIES FROM THE GOLDEN AGE *reflect the words and expressions used in the 1930s and 1940s, adding unique flavor and authenticity to the tales. While a character's speech may often reflect regional origins, it also can convey attitudes common in the day. So that readers can better grasp such cultural and historical terms, uncommon words or expressions of the era, the following glossary has been provided.*

aileron: a hinged flap on the trailing edge of an aircraft wing, used to control banking movements.

Akron **and** *Macon:* two rigid airships built in the United States for the US Navy and first flown in the early 1930s. Often referred to as flying aircraft carriers, each ship carried biplanes which could be launched and recovered in flight by means of a hook assembly. This greatly extended the range over with the *Akron* and *Macon* could scout the open sea for enemy vessels.

altimeter: a gauge that measures altitude.

amphib: amphibian; an airplane designed for taking off from and landing on both land and water.

• GLOSSARY •

beam: an early form of radio navigation using beacons to define navigational airways. A pilot flew for 100 miles guided by the beacon behind him and then tuned in the beacon ahead for the next 100 miles. The beacons transmitted two Morse code signals, the letter "A" and the letter "N." When the aircraft was centered on the airway, these two signals merged into a steady, monotonous tone. If the aircraft drifted off course to one side, the Morse code for the letter "A" could be faintly heard. Straying to the opposite side produced the "N" Morse code signal. Used figuratively.

blackjack: coerce by pressure.

Bolling: Bolling Field; located in southwest Washington, DC and officially opened in 1918, it was named in honor of the first high-ranking air service officer killed in World War I. Bolling served as a research and testing ground for new aviation equipment and its first mission provided aerial defense of the capital.

bus: slang for automobile.

cabane: a framework supporting the wings of an airplane.

cabin job: an airplane that has an enclosed section where passengers can sit or cargo is stored.

Charleston: a city and seaport of southeast South Carolina; a major commercial and cultural center since colonial times.

davits: any of various cranelike devices, used singly or in pairs, for supporting, raising and lowering boats, anchors and cargo over a hatchway or side of a ship.

Department of Commerce: the department of the US federal government that promotes and administers domestic and foreign commerce. In 1926, Congress passed an Air

• GLOSSARY •

Commerce Act that gave the US Department of Commerce some regulation over air facilities, the authority to establish air traffic rules and the authority to issue licenses and certificates.

dope: a type of lacquer formerly used to protect, waterproof and stretch tight the cloth surfaces of airplane wings.

egg: slang for fellow or guy.

frigate birds: large black seabirds with powerful wings, forked tails and long hooked beaks; they are native to tropical waters.

G-men: government men; agents of the Federal Bureau of Investigation.

gunwale: the upper edge of the side of a boat. Originally a gunwale was a platform where guns were mounted, and was designed to accommodate the additional stresses imposed by the artillery being used.

hash house: an inexpensive eating place.

Havana: a seaport in and the capital of Cuba, on the northwest coast.

hinterland: the remote or less developed parts of a country; back country.

iron men: men of unusual physical endurance.

jury strut: small subsidiary struts that provide extra attachment between the main strut and the wing. They steady main wing struts to eliminate unwanted vibration, and also help to provide additional support of the main strut when the aircraft is experiencing different air pressures.

Keys: Florida Keys; a chain of approximately 1,700 islands beginning at the southeastern tip of the Florida peninsula

• GLOSSARY •

and extending in a gentle arc to Key West, the westernmost of the inhabited islands. Key West is just ninety-eight miles from Cuba.

L'Enfant: Pierre Charles L'Enfant (1754–1825), French-born US engineer, architect and urban planner best known for designing the layout of the streets in Washington, DC. After studying in Paris, he volunteered as a soldier and engineer in the American Revolutionary Army. Congress made him major of engineers in 1783. In 1791, George Washington had him prepare a plan for a federal capital on the Potomac River, which was later generally followed in the construction of Washington, DC.

leeward: situated away from the wind, or on the side of something, especially a boat, that is away or sheltered from the wind.

mailed fists: armed or overbearing forces.

monoplane: an airplane with only one main supporting surface or one set of wings.

Pensacola: city and seaport on Pensacola Bay in northwest Florida. Noted for the US naval air station established there in 1914.

Potomac: a river in the east central United States; it begins in the Appalachian Mountains in West Virginia and flows eastward to the Chesapeake Bay, forming the boundary between Maryland and Virginia.

roadster: an open-top automobile with a single seat in front for two or three persons, a fabric top and either a luggage compartment or a rumble seat in back. A rumble seat is

· GLOSSARY ·

an upholstered exterior seat with a hinged lid that opens to form the back of the seat when in use.

rudder: a device used to steer ships or aircraft. A rudder is a flat plane or sheet of material attached with hinges to the craft's stern or tail. In typical aircraft, pedals operate rudders via mechanical linkages.

Scheherazade: the female narrator of *The Arabian Nights,* who during one thousand and one adventurous nights saved her life by entertaining her husband, the king, with stories.

scud cloud: small, ragged, low cloud fragments that are unattached to a larger cloud base at first and are often seen with and behind cold fronts and thunderstorm gust fronts.

struts: supports for a structure such as an aircraft wing, roof or bridge.

tarmac: airport runway.

up-toiling: proceeding upward laboriously or with difficulty.

Very pistol: a special pistol that shoots Very lights, a variety of colored signal flares.

volplaning: gliding toward the earth in an airplane, with no motor power or with the power shut off.

windjammer: a sailing vessel, especially one equipped with many large sails and capable of making fast voyages.

zero-zero: (of atmospheric conditions) having or characterized by zero visibility in both horizontal and vertical directions. Used figuratively.

L. Ron Hubbard
in the Golden Age
of Pulp Fiction

*In writing an adventure story
a writer has to know that he is adventuring
for a lot of people who cannot.
The writer has to take them here and there
about the globe and show them
excitement and love and realism.
As long as that writer is living the part of an
adventurer when he is hammering
the keys, he is succeeding with his story.*

*Adventuring is a state of mind.
If you adventure through life, you have a
good chance to be a success on paper.*

*Adventure doesn't mean globe-trotting,
exactly, and it doesn't mean great deeds.
Adventuring is like art.
You have to live it to make it real.*

—L. RON HUBBARD

L. Ron Hubbard and American Pulp Fiction

BORN March 13, 1911, L. Ron Hubbard lived a life at least as expansive as the stories with which he enthralled a hundred million readers through a fifty-year career.

Originally hailing from Tilden, Nebraska, he spent his formative years in a classically rugged Montana, replete with the cowpunchers, lawmen and desperadoes who would later people his Wild West adventures. And lest anyone imagine those adventures were drawn from vicarious experience, he was not only breaking broncs at a tender age, he was also among the few whites ever admitted into Blackfoot society as a bona fide blood brother. While if only to round out an otherwise rough and tumble youth, his mother was that rarity of her time—a thoroughly educated woman—who introduced her son to the classics of Occidental literature even before his seventh birthday.

But as any dedicated L. Ron Hubbard reader will attest, his world extended far beyond Montana. In point of fact, and as the son of a United States naval officer, by the age of eighteen he had traveled over a quarter of a million miles. Included therein were three Pacific crossings to a then still mysterious Asia, where he ran with the likes of Her British Majesty's agent-in-place for North China, and the last in the line of Royal Magicians from the court of Kublai Khan. For the record, L. Ron Hubbard was also among the first Westerners to gain admittance to forbidden Tibetan monasteries below Manchuria, and his photographs of China's Great Wall long graced American geography texts.

L. Ron Hubbard, left, at Congressional Airport, Washington, DC, 1931, with members of George Washington University flying club.

Upon his return to the United States and a hasty completion of his interrupted high school education, the young Ron Hubbard entered George Washington University. There, as fans of his aerial adventures may have heard, he earned his wings as a pioneering barnstormer at the dawn of American aviation. He also earned a place in free-flight record books for the longest sustained flight above Chicago. Moreover, as a roving reporter for *Sportsman Pilot* (featuring his first professionally penned articles), he further helped inspire a generation of pilots who would take America to world airpower.

Immediately beyond his sophomore year, Ron embarked on the first of his famed ethnological expeditions, initially to then untrammeled Caribbean shores (descriptions of which would later fill a whole series of West Indies mystery-thrillers). That the Puerto Rican interior would also figure into the future of Ron Hubbard stories was likewise no accident. For in addition to cultural studies of the island, a 1932–33

LRH expedition is rightly remembered as conducting the first complete mineralogical survey of a Puerto Rico under United States jurisdiction.

There was many another adventure along this vein: As a lifetime member of the famed Explorers Club, L. Ron Hubbard charted North Pacific waters with the first shipboard radio direction finder, and so pioneered a long-range navigation system universally employed until the late twentieth century. While not to put too fine an edge on it, he also held a rare Master Mariner's license to pilot any vessel, of any tonnage in any ocean.

Yet lest we stray too far afield, there is an LRH note at this juncture in his saga, and it reads in part:

"I started out writing for the pulps, writing the best I knew, writing for every mag on the stands, slanting as well as I could."

To which one might add: His earliest submissions date from the summer of 1934, and included tales drawn from true-to-life Asian adventures, with characters roughly modeled on British/American intelligence operatives he had known in Shanghai. His early Westerns were similarly peppered with details drawn from personal experience. Although therein lay a first hard lesson from the often cruel world of the pulps. His first Westerns were soundly rejected as lacking the authenticity of a Max Brand yarn

Capt. L. Ron Hubbard in Ketchikan, Alaska, 1940, on his Alaskan Radio Experimental Expedition, the first of three voyages conducted under the Explorers Club flag.

(a particularly frustrating comment given L. Ron Hubbard's Westerns came straight from his Montana homeland, while Max Brand was a mediocre New York poet named Frederick Schiller Faust, who turned out implausible six-shooter tales from the terrace of an Italian villa).

Nevertheless, and needless to say, L. Ron Hubbard persevered and soon earned a reputation as among the most publishable names in pulp fiction, with a ninety percent placement rate of first-draft manuscripts. He was also among the most prolific, averaging between seventy and a hundred thousand words a month. Hence the rumors that L. Ron Hubbard had redesigned a typewriter for faster keyboard action and pounded out manuscripts on a continuous roll of butcher paper to save the precious seconds it took to insert a single sheet of paper into manual typewriters of the day.

That all L. Ron Hubbard stories did not run beneath said byline is yet another aspect of pulp fiction lore. That is, as publishers periodically rejected manuscripts from top-drawer authors if only to avoid paying top dollar, L. Ron Hubbard and company just as frequently replied with submissions under various pseudonyms. In Ron's case, the

> **A MAN OF MANY NAMES**
>
> *Between 1934 and 1950, L. Ron Hubbard authored more than fifteen million words of fiction in more than two hundred classic publications. To supply his fans and editors with stories across an array of genres and pulp titles, he adopted fifteen pseudonyms in addition to his already renowned L. Ron Hubbard byline.*
>
> Winchester Remington Colt
> Lt. Jonathan Daly
> Capt. Charles Gordon
> Capt. L. Ron Hubbard
> Bernard Hubbel
> Michael Keith
> Rene Lafayette
> Legionnaire 148
> Legionnaire 14830
> Ken Martin
> Scott Morgan
> Lt. Scott Morgan
> Kurt von Rachen
> Barry Randolph
> Capt. Humbert Reynolds

• AMERICAN PULP FICTION •

list included: Rene Lafayette, Captain Charles Gordon, Lt. Scott Morgan and the notorious Kurt von Rachen—supposedly on the lam for a murder rap, while hammering out two-fisted prose in Argentina. The point: While L. Ron Hubbard as Ken Martin spun stories of Southeast Asian intrigue, LRH as Barry Randolph authored tales of romance on the Western range—which, stretching between a dozen genres is how he came to stand among the two hundred elite authors providing close to a million tales through the glory days of American Pulp Fiction.

L. Ron Hubbard, circa 1930, at the outset of a literary career that would finally span half a century.

In evidence of exactly that, by 1936 L. Ron Hubbard was literally leading pulp fiction's elite as president of New York's American Fiction Guild. Members included a veritable pulp hall of fame: Lester "Doc Savage" Dent, Walter "The Shadow" Gibson, and the legendary Dashiell Hammett—to cite but a few.

Also in evidence of just where L. Ron Hubbard stood within his first two years on the American pulp circuit: By the spring of 1937, he was ensconced in Hollywood, adopting a Caribbean thriller for Columbia Pictures, remembered today as *The Secret of Treasure Island*. Comprising fifteen thirty-minute episodes, the L. Ron Hubbard screenplay led to the most profitable matinée serial in Hollywood history. In accord with Hollywood culture, he was thereafter continually called upon

• L. RON HUBBARD •

to rewrite/doctor scripts—most famously for long-time friend and fellow adventurer Clark Gable.

In the interim—and herein lies another distinctive chapter of the L. Ron Hubbard story—he continually worked to open Pulp Kingdom gates to up-and-coming authors. Or, for that matter, anyone who wished to write. It was a fairly unconventional stance, as markets were already thin and competition razor sharp. But the fact remains, it was an L. Ron Hubbard hallmark that he vehemently lobbied on behalf of young authors—regularly supplying instructional articles to trade journals, guest-lecturing to short story classes at George Washington University and Harvard, and even founding his own creative writing competition. It was established in 1940, dubbed the Golden Pen, and guaranteed winners both New York representation and publication in *Argosy*.

The 1937 Secret of Treasure Island, *a fifteen-episode serial adapted for the screen by L. Ron Hubbard from his novel,* Murder at Pirate Castle.

But it was John W. Campbell Jr.'s *Astounding Science Fiction* that finally proved the most memorable LRH vehicle. While every fan of L. Ron Hubbard's galactic epics undoubtedly knows the story, it nonetheless bears repeating: By late 1938, the pulp publishing magnate of Street & Smith was determined to revamp *Astounding Science Fiction* for broader readership. In particular, senior editorial director F. Orlin Tremaine called for stories with a stronger *human element*. When acting editor John W. Campbell balked, preferring his spaceship-driven tales, Tremaine enlisted Hubbard. Hubbard, in turn, replied with the genre's first truly *character-driven* works, wherein heroes are pitted not against bug-eyed monsters but the mystery and majesty of deep space itself—and thus was launched the Golden Age of Science Fiction.

The names alone are enough to quicken the pulse of any science fiction aficionado, including LRH friend and protégé, Robert Heinlein, Isaac Asimov, A. E. van Vogt and Ray Bradbury. Moreover, when coupled with LRH stories of fantasy, we further come to what's rightly been described as the foundation of every modern tale of horror: L. Ron Hubbard's immortal *Fear*. It was rightly proclaimed by Stephen King as one of the very few works to genuinely warrant that overworked term "classic"—as in: *"This is a classic tale of creeping, surreal menace and horror.... This is one of the really, really good ones."*

To accommodate the greater body of L. Ron Hubbard fantasies, Street & Smith inaugurated *Unknown*—a classic pulp if there ever was one, and wherein readers were soon thrilling to the likes of *Typewriter in the Sky* and *Slaves of Sleep* of which Frederik Pohl would declare: *"There are bits and pieces from Ron's work that became part of the language in ways that very few other writers managed."*

L. Ron Hubbard, 1948, among fellow science fiction luminaries at the World Science Fiction Convention in Toronto.

And, indeed, at J. W. Campbell Jr.'s insistence, Ron was regularly drawing on themes from the Arabian Nights and so introducing readers to a world of genies, jinn, Aladdin and Sinbad—all of which, of course, continue to float through cultural mythology to this day.

At least as influential in terms of post-apocalypse stories was L. Ron Hubbard's 1940 *Final Blackout*. Generally acclaimed as the finest anti-war novel of the decade and among the ten best works of the genre ever authored—here, too, was a tale that would live on in ways few other writers imagined.

Hence, the later Robert Heinlein verdict: "Final Blackout *is as perfect a piece of science fiction as has ever been written.*"

Like many another who both lived and wrote American pulp adventure, the war proved a tragic end to Ron's sojourn in the pulps. He served with distinction in four theaters and was highly decorated for commanding corvettes in the North Pacific. He was also grievously wounded in combat, lost many a close friend and colleague and thus resolved to say farewell to pulp fiction and devote himself to what it had supported these many years—namely, his serious research.

Portland, Oregon, 1943; L. Ron Hubbard, captain of the US Navy subchaser PC 815.

But in no way was the LRH literary saga at an end, for as he wrote some thirty years later, in 1980:

"Recently there came a period when I had little to do. This was novel in a life so crammed with busy years, and I decided to amuse myself by writing a novel that was pure *science fiction."*

♦ AMERICAN PULP FICTION ♦

That work was *Battlefield Earth: A Saga of the Year 3000*. It was an immediate *New York Times* bestseller and, in fact, the first international science fiction blockbuster in decades. It was not, however, L. Ron Hubbard's magnum opus, as that distinction is generally reserved for his next and final work: The 1.2 million word *Mission Earth*.

> **Final Blackout** *is as perfect a piece of science fiction as has ever been written.*
>
> —Robert Heinlein

How he managed those 1.2 million words in just over twelve months is yet another piece of the L. Ron Hubbard legend. But the fact remains, he did indeed author a ten-volume *dekalogy* that lives in publishing history for the fact that each and every volume of the series was also a *New York Times* bestseller.

Moreover, as subsequent generations discovered L. Ron Hubbard through republished works and novelizations of his screenplays, the mere fact of his name on a cover signaled an international bestseller. . . . Until, to date, sales of his works exceed hundreds of millions, and he otherwise remains among the most enduring and widely read authors in literary history. Although as a final word on the tales of L. Ron Hubbard, perhaps it's enough to simply reiterate what editors told readers in the glory days of American Pulp Fiction:

He writes the way he does, brothers, because he's been there, seen it and done it!

THE STORIES FROM THE GOLDEN AGE

Your ticket to adventure starts here with the Stories from the Golden Age collection by master storyteller L. Ron Hubbard. These gripping tales are set in a kaleidoscope of exotic locales and brim with fascinating characters, including some of the most vile villains, dangerous dames and brazen heroes you'll ever get to meet.

The entire collection of over one hundred and fifty stories is being released in a series of eighty books and audiobooks. For an up-to-date listing of available titles, go to www.goldenagestories.com.

AIR ADVENTURE

Arctic Wings
The Battling Pilot
Boomerang Bomber
The Crate Killer
The Dive Bomber
Forbidden Gold
Hurtling Wings
The Lieutenant Takes the Sky

Man-Killers of the Air
On Blazing Wings
Red Death Over China
Sabotage in the Sky
Sky Birds Dare!
The Sky-Crasher
Trouble on His Wings
Wings Over Ethiopia

• STORIES FROM THE GOLDEN AGE •

FAR-FLUNG ADVENTURE

The Adventure of "X"
All Frontiers Are Jealous
The Barbarians
The Black Sultan
Black Towers to Danger
The Bold Dare All
Buckley Plays a Hunch
The Cossack
Destiny's Drum
Escape for Three
Fifty-Fifty O'Brien
The Headhunters
Hell's Legionnaire
He Walked to War
Hostage to Death
Hurricane
The Iron Duke
Machine Gun 21,000
Medals for Mahoney
Price of a Hat
Red Sand
The Sky Devil
The Small Boss of Nunaloha
The Squad That Never Came Back
Starch and Stripes
Tomb of the Ten Thousand Dead
Trick Soldier
While Bugles Blow!
Yukon Madness

SEA ADVENTURE

Cargo of Coffins
The Drowned City
False Cargo
Grounded
Loot of the Shanung
Mister Tidwell, Gunner
The Phantom Patrol
Sea Fangs
Submarine
Twenty Fathoms Down
Under the Black Ensign

• STORIES FROM THE GOLDEN AGE •

TALES FROM THE ORIENT

The Devil—With Wings *Pearl Pirate*
The Falcon Killer *The Red Dragon*
Five Mex for a Million *Spy Killer*
Golden Hell *Tah*
The Green God *The Trail of the Red Diamonds*
Hurricane's Roar *Wind-Gone-Mad*
Inky Odds *Yellow Loot*
Orders Is Orders

MYSTERY

The Blow Torch Murder *The Grease Spot*
Brass Keys to Murder *Killer Ape*
Calling Squad Cars! *Killer's Law*
The Carnival of Death *The Mad Dog Murder*
The Chee-Chalker *Mouthpiece*
Dead Men Kill *Murder Afloat*
The Death Flyer *The Slickers*
Flame City *They Killed Him Dead*

FANTASY

Borrowed Glory *If I Were You*
The Crossroads *The Last Drop*
Danger in the Dark *The Room*
The Devil's Rescue *The Tramp*
He Didn't Like Cats

SCIENCE FICTION

The Automagic Horse *A Matter of Matter*
Battle of Wizards *The Obsolete Weapon*
Battling Bolto *One Was Stubborn*
The Beast *The Planet Makers*
Beyond All Weapons *The Professor Was a Thief*
A Can of Vacuum *The Slaver*
The Conroy Diary *Space Can*
The Dangerous Dimension *Strain*
Final Enemy *Tough Old Man*
The Great Secret *240,000 Miles Straight Up*
Greed *When Shadows Fall*
The Invaders

• STORIES FROM THE GOLDEN AGE •

WESTERN

The Baron of Coyote River
Blood on His Spurs
Boss of the Lazy B
Branded Outlaw
Cattle King for a Day
Come and Get It
Death Waits at Sundown
Devil's Manhunt
The Ghost Town Gun-Ghost
Gun Boss of Tumbleweed
Gunman!
Gunman's Tally
The Gunner from Gehenna
Hoss Tamer
Johnny, the Town Tamer
King of the Gunmen
The Magic Quirt
Man for Breakfast
The No-Gun Gunhawk
The No-Gun Man
The Ranch That No One Would Buy
Reign of the Gila Monster
Ride 'Em, Cowboy
Ruin at Rio Piedras
Shadows from Boot Hill
Silent Pards
Six-Gun Caballero
Stacked Bullets
Stranger in Town
Tinhorn's Daughter
The Toughest Ranger
Under the Diehard Brand
Vengeance Is Mine!
When Gilhooly Was in Flower

Your Next Ticket to Adventure

Delve into the Heat of the Action!

Johnny Brice is a hotheaded, hard-working "picture-chaser" for the newsreels. He loves to fly into the mouth of danger (whether forest fire, shipwreck or flood), get the story first, shoot it and send the film back fast so that it can be turned into newsreels for theaters all across America. He's the best there ever was as a "top dog" reporter ... up till the day he inadvertently saves the life of a golden-haired girl he pulls out of the ocean while covering a ship burning at sea.

The dame, or "Jinx," as Brice calls her, seems to bring bad luck like a black cat under a ladder. She keeps Brice on his toes and waist-deep in trouble as they trek the globe from Idaho to the Orient, chasing pictures for the World News. Trouble is, no matter how hard he tries or how good the story, Johnny can't seem to get good shots ... nor can he shake the girl.

Get
Trouble on His Wings

PAPERBACK OR AUDIOBOOK: $9.95 EACH
Free Shipping & Handling for Book Club Members
CALL TOLL-FREE: 1-877-8GALAXY (1-877-842-5299)
OR GO ONLINE TO **www.goldenagestories.com**

Galaxy Press, 7051 Hollywood Blvd., Suite 200, Hollywood, CA 90028

JOIN THE PULP REVIVAL
America in the 1930s and 40s

Pulp fiction was in its heyday and 30 million readers were regularly riveted by the larger-than-life tales of master storyteller L. Ron Hubbard. For this was pulp fiction's golden age, when the writing was raw and every page packed a walloping punch.

That magic can now be yours. An evocative world of nefarious villains, exotic intrigues, courageous heroes and heroines—a world that today's cinema has barely tapped for tales of adventure and swashbucklers.

Enroll today in the Stories from the Golden Age Club and begin receiving your monthly feature edition selected from more than 150 stories in the collection.

You may choose to enjoy them as either a paperback or audiobook for the special membership price of $9.95 each month along with FREE shipping and handling.

CALL TOLL-FREE: 1-877-8GALAXY
(1-877-842-5299) OR GO ONLINE TO
www.goldenagestories.com
AND BECOME PART OF THE PULP REVIVAL!

Prices are set in US dollars only. For non-US residents, please call 1-323-466-7815 for pricing information. Free shipping available for US residents only.

Galaxy Press, 7051 Hollywood Blvd., Suite 200, Hollywood, CA 90028